RED IN THE MORNING

JERRY FARNHAM

Red in the Morning Copyright © 2024 Jerry Farnham

This is a work of fiction. Names, characters, places, and incidents either are the product of the author's imagination or are used fictitiously, and any resemblance to actual living persons, events, or locales is entirely coincidental.

Published by the author
Edited by Pat Cole
Cover Art by Bryan Soeres
Interior Design by Eric H. Bowen
Body Text set in TeX Gyre Pagella 10 point

ISBN: 979-8-218-98778-7

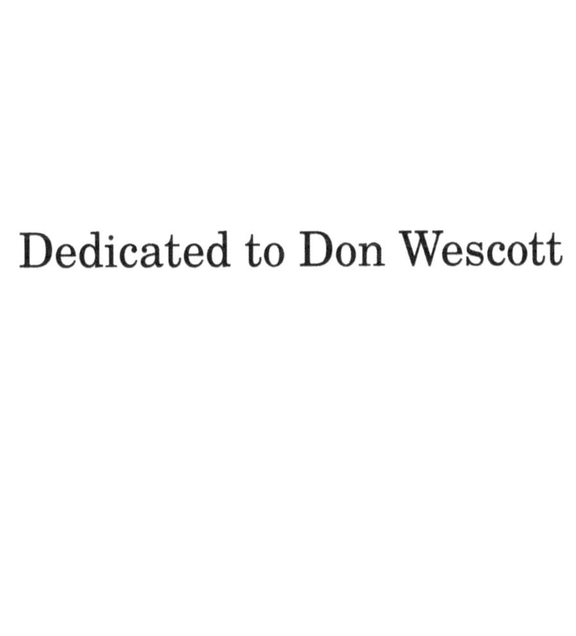

Dedicated to Don Wescott

Acknowledgments

Where do I even begin? The support I have received since the release of the first book can't be described without sounding like I ate a thesaurus. To all my readers, I say thank you for purchasing a book and supporting me. Andy Roberts started helping me on this journey before the paperbacks were printed. He has helped me navigate this new world I find myself in. A special thanks to my followers on Facebook, especially to those that share my posts: Julie Murphy, Darrell Gudroe, Sarah Edith Foster, and I know there are more. You guys certainly help spread the word.

Regarding getting the word out, thank you to Rob Caldwell and 207, Lisa Kristoff, and the Boothbay Register. I would also like to thank Krista Nadeau and Jon Johansson for their interviews and articles. The press you gave me helped push my first book to a higher level of exposure.

For this book I had a new batch of beta readers: Joanne Allen, Jen Reiter, Darrell Gudroe, Robert Watts, and another silent reader. Thanks for the time, the input, the help, and your honesty.

D&G Machine has had my back for this entire endeavor. Approving of time-off to go to book signings and author talks, and the guys on the floor asking how the book is doing and when will the next one be out. Thanks guys.

Cover art done by the talented Bryan Soeres and formatted by the ever so patient Ruth Lowell at Time Bouys.

Thank you to my wife and kids for being so patient with time missed at home. Love you.

The cost of printing is a huge burden, it's expensive, and stressful. I did another pre-purchase campaign this time around and it worked again, although there was a time I didn't think it was going to work. First person to mention in my pre-purchase campaign is Darrell Gudroe, he not only made some moving posts to motivate buyers but got in contact with multiple businesses. Darrell, thanks again man. Both Kaler's and Brady's restaurants pitched in and bought multiple pre-purchase hardcovers. I am telling you, if you are in Boothbay Harbor, you absolutely need to stop and get someting to eat and drink at these restarants, never know, you may even run into your favorite blue collar Maine author!

Hard cover pre-purchasers are as follows: Frederick Farnham (Dad), Michelle Farnham (Mom), Fredrica Luke, Colin Stokes, Betsy Lowe, Darrell Gudroe, Michael Morris (Mr. DuraBrite), Vickie Colby, Elise Cundy, Kelly Smith, Caleb Hodgdon, Clive Farrin (the same person that is in both books) Sam Kaler (Kaler's Restaurant), Melanie Hibbard, Jack Sherman, and Jennie Plumber (Brady's Restaurant)

Paperback pre-purchasers are as follows: Megan Gill, Patti Corscaden, Dianne Barter, Crystal Burch, Nicholas Martin in memory of his grandfather(Herbert G Martin), Kim Burnham, Fredrica Luke, Michelle Farnham (Mom), Brett Murphy, Linda Swanson, Pete Merrow, Sarah Baldwin, Charlene Gajewsk, Charles Julian, Joanne Allen (Beta Reader), Meg Donaldson, Rachel Fecteau, Fran Lofland, Hillary Barret, Maureen Collard, Venessa Herman, and Andy Roberts.

Donations made by: Fred Farnham, Brady's, Kaler's, Anthony Kotoun, Fred Scott, and Lisa Kristoff

Last but certainly not least. The mystery man in the corner at my author talks. The guy milling around at my signings. My driver, friend, and father-in-law. Don Wescott, this book is dedicated to you.

Preface

To write this book, I had to delve into the minds of human traffickers. Nothing made me want to punch my computer screen and go take a shower more. Folks, it's here. It's not just in other countries, it's here in the USA and yeah, it's here in Maine.

Are you still with me? Good, I didn't dwell too much on the subject, but I did peel back some layers and let people know how it happens and what happens to the victims. You will still find as much comedy, values, and charm that you found in my first book, Red At Night. Just remember there is one part of the book I didn't enjoy writing, but I needed to drive the message home.

Also, you will find a character in the book, Tylar Michaud, his name is not a typo. He existed. He was a young man that was lost at sea August of 2023. Go ahead and Google him, I will wait….. You back? Yeah, that is the reality of growing up here in the lobstering community. Fair winds and following seas Tylar.

Again, this book is not all gloom and doom. Russell will get you laughing before you know it.

DAMARISCOTTA RIVER
BOOTHBAY HARBOR
HEAD OF THE BAY
EAST BOOTHBAY
LOBSTER COVE
BOOTHBAY HARBOR
CABBAGE ISLAND
LINEKIN BAY
MOUSE ISLAND
SPRUCE POINT
BURNT ISLAND
OCEAN POINT
SOUTHPORT ISLAND
SQUIRREL ISLAND
DAMARISCOVE ISLAND
DAMARISCOVE HARBOR
N
W
E
S

Chapter 1

Carla Rand had been sitting at McSeagull's bar, waiting on Dan Ross. She hoped Dan would appreciate the fact she dressed up for him; she never wore dresses or skirts, and rarely wore make-up. For tonight, she had bought a nice casual dress and had even done her hair rather than just tossing it into a ponytail. She swirled the red wine in the glass as she looked out and saw Jack's boat idling out through the harbor, and figured he and Melissa were out for a romantic boat ride. Romance had been something that had eluded her for so long. A few boyfriends here and there, but nothing lasted. Being a DEA agent did a good job of hindering a relationship. Not to mention, most men didn't appreciate her job being more masculine than theirs. Dan wouldn't have that problem. He knew her job, and with him retiring soon, it would work well.

She was getting ahead of herself. This was their first date; no reason to think long term,……yet. It was funny he wasn't here yet. Dan was always on time — on time…. early. Dan lived by the motto "early is on time, and on time is late." She glanced at her watch, and it made her stomach turn. Something had to be wrong.

Dan Ross opened his right eye. His left was swollen shut. He could see blood smeared all over the plastic sheathing that had been spread out on the floor. His blood garnished with his teeth. His hands and legs were zip-tied to a chair that had chafe marks from many Zip-ties.

"Mr. Ross, please let us end this ugliness. I can put a bullet in your head, and you will be done. Just tell me why Agent Rand is still investigating me after she was told not to. You said you would take care of it. You said the visit from my friends posing as FSB (Russian Federal Security Service, or Federalnaya Sluzhba Bezopastnosti) would be enough to make her leave us alone. I didn't kill the guards at the jail, as you requested. I paid you very well to make sure she would stop chasing my tail; meanwhile, it seems you are chasing her's," Demitrie Balfour said, while looking at the incoming messages from Carla Rand on Dan Ross's phone.

Dan's head hurt.... hell, his whole body hurt. They had been working him over for hours now, or at least it felt that way. As much as he hurt, one thing was clear — his regret. Of all the time in the FBI, he had seen many criminals come to the realization they had messed up. He now was having that revelation. He remembered when Demitre Balfour first approached him; he went by Robert then. Some DEA agent was hot on the trail of his competition. He saw this as an opportunity to eliminate competition and safely move drugs and guns into Russia. His role was to push the DEA agent in the direction of Katyana and Casmere. After the big bust, Balfour would break free, then send some of his people over, posing as FSB. Ross would sign the case over to them. They would take the drugs and guns to Russia. It all would have worked well too, if Carla hadn't kept digging. She was so proud of herself when she had called him with the news that the FSB guys were not legit and the shipment to Russia had been stopped. He could remember his dizziness and nauseousness when she told him. It had been a few long weeks since then. A lot of checking behind him, constantly looking out, nervously going about a normal day worried someone would pop out of nowhere with a gun, or bomb going off, or anything. This afternoon, while in Portland finishing up his retirement paperwork at the FBI office, he noticed a black van following him while he was walking back to his truck. But the black van was what they wanted him to see. While looking back at it, he ran into someone. He felt a sharp pain in his back. Then he woke up here. Zip-tied to a chair. Mr. Balfour walked out from behind him. The tall, large man with his black hair and black eyes looked down at Dan Ross, much like a predator looks at prey when it knows there is nothing the prey can do. Mr. Balfour glanced up and nodded at someone. A giant man stepped out and punched him in the stomach and chest, nonstop hitting him in the torso. Mr. Balfour motioned for his associate to stop. He paused for several minutes. Dan figured it was to let him catch his breath because that's when the questions started. With every answer he gave that Balfour didn't like came a hit to the head. He had been knocked out a couple times, but they would wake him up. He honestly did not know what Carla had on them. She may have told him tonight. He heard his phone's message tone again.

"Well, Mr. Ross, looks like your little date isn't going to happen. She just texted that she is leaving the restaurant, and she will call tomorrow. Sorry I have interfered with your love life. I think after we are done with you, we will be taking a little trip up to Boothbay Harbor and visit Agent Rand. We will show her the same hospitality we have shown you. Now here is your last chance to tell us what she has on us. If you do, I will personally put a bullet in your head, and this will be over. If not, my friends here will use you for batting practice," he said while putting his phone back in Dan's breast pocket.

He was too weak to cry, even though he wanted to. This was not how he wanted this to end. The worst part was, he really didn't know anything. If he did, he would gladly tell them. Looking at the two thugs with baseball bats made him crave that bullet. "I don't know anything.... really", he pleaded. With every painful hit, a piece of hope went away. After a dozen or so hits, he couldn't feel them anymore. They made sure not to hit him in the head so as to make it last as long as possible. In the end, he couldn't breathe and slowly and painfully slipped out of consciousness.

Balfour motioned for his men to stop. He looked down at the bloody mass of Dan Ross's body. It wasn't the first time he had done this, and it certainly wasn't going to be his last. The gargling of his breathing stopped. He probably still had a heartbeat but not for much longer.

"Wrap him up in plastic and put him in a truck. We can be in Boothbay Harbor in an hour. You will drop him off the same dock that started this whole mess. When he is found, they will ID him, and Agent Rand will definitely be notified. After seeing him like this, she will be more cooperative than he. If not…. more batting practice or whatever you two want to do with her for fun."

The two men wrapped Dan Ross's body in plastic. The movement of the Agent caused more gargling and even moaning. "The poor son of a bitch is still alive. Should we finish him?" One of the two men asked.

"No, let him go slowly. He deserves it," Damitri said.

They placed him in the back of the truck. One of Dan's hands flopped out of the plastic. With every last bit of energy Dan could muster in his battered, dying body, he managed to slide his hand out far enough to the edge of the box truck. Trying to pull himself out, but that was it, his life slipped away, and the gate came down on his hand.

❧❧❧❧❧❧❧

"Pregnant…you're pregnant…how I mean…what…" Jack stammered, trying to find the right words.

"Well, Jack, do we need to have the birds and the bees talk? Do you still want to marry me? Melissa asked, not quite sure of her emotions.

"Yes, of course. I just figured we were…. safe."

"Well, the pill is 99% effective, but I am human and sometimes…."

"Wow…I am going to be a father." Said Jack, now sitting next to Melissa on the warm engine box.

"And a husband."

"How far along…or how long…?"

"I did a home test two weeks ago and another this morning. I am going to schedule an appointment with a doctor to get the official test. I want you to go with me."

Jack's heart was beating heavily now. The shock of it had passed, and now the thoughts of being a dad buzzed through his head. "I am going to be a dad."

"And a husband…" Melissa reminded him again.

Jack smiled and turned to her. "Yes, a husband. Your husband, and you are going to be my wife."

They kissed passionately and held each other. They staring out into the night sky and the flat calm water and breathed the salt air.

"So, what do we tell people?" Jack asked.

"Well, we can tell them I asked you to marry me, and you said yes. As far as me being pregnant, I want to talk to your mother first. Maybe after a month or two we can tell others."

"What about the media?"

"We can let them find things out for themselves. No need to feed them info."

"We really suck at taking it slow, don't we?"

"Yes, but we are good at other things," she said with a flirty smile.

"Apparently so," Jack said with a laugh.

As Jack sat there holding Melissa, he daydreamed about his future kid. Would it be a boy or girl? It didn't matter to him as long as it was healthy, though he found himself hoping for a girl. He remembered watching Michael with Lizzy. Michael sitting in a tiny chair attending a tea party, pretending to drink tea and nibble on cupcakes. Watching Michael deal with the anxiety of preparing Lizzy for college. "It will be worth it," he thought to himself. Melissa was bouncing back and forth between joy, self-doubt, and anxiety about what was to come. With the relationship she and her mother had, how could she be a mom herself? She enjoyed working with kids, but all the ones she had worked with were teenagers. She would soon be responsible for another human's life. Then there was marrying Jack. She had been dreaming of marrying him since their first kiss. She had thought they would spend some time together before having kids. Now they would be newlyweds and parents all at the same time. The slight moment of doubt was overcome by her confidence in her and Jack's bond. They could do it; they would do it. They would raise a child as husband and wife. The Finn family was about to get a little bigger.

Russell got up from his chair and headed to the bedroom. After a few steps, he felt dizzy and had to grab the door frame to steady himself. Anne looked up from her book and saw him with a distant look on his face.

"Russell, are you ok?"

"Yeah…just got up too quick. I have been a little short on breath lately. Probably got a bug coming on."

"Never seen you look like that before. Maybe you should see Dr. Long."

"Christ, Anne, I ain't running to the doctor every time I get a cold. They have better things to do than that," Russell snapped back while getting into bed.

"Russell Finn, you old ox, don't talk to me that way. I am concerned. You have been coughing and wheezing for more than a month. I don't think it's a simple cold. Go to the doctor and have him take a look at you. If not for yourself, do it for me."

"That's a low blow, Anne…do it for me…I will go see him if it makes you happy."

Anne, taking the win gracefully, decided not to keep harping on the matter. Russell had not been himself for a while. Along with the coughing and wheezing, he seemed to have less energy. When they first got The Harbor, Russell was a ball of energy. Working late into the evenings, fixing things here and there. Lately, she had caught him sitting down more, and simple tasks seem to take longer. She knew he was getting older, but this was different. "Probably nothing serious" is what she told herself as she dozed off to sleep.

⁕⁂⁕

Sergeant Brian O'Niel of the Maine State Police was just starting his night shift. Merging onto 95 to get to his favorite spot for monitoring highway speed, he found himself behind a big box truck with Maine plates. As usual, the truck was going over the speed limit, but nothing crazy. It never failed, though, to have the driver panic at the sight of a police car behind them and slow down to the actual speed limit. The driver really must have panicked this time because he slowed down so abruptly that it caught Brian by surprise. After checking his driver side mirror quickly, Brian decided to pass the box truck rather than slow down. Halfway into his lane change to pass the truck, Brian's eyes moved back from the mirror to the back of the truck; something sticking out from the tailgate of the truck caught his attention. He jerked the wheel quickly to get back behind the truck instead of passing it.

Inside the truck, the two men were checking the mirrors. They were hoping the cop would just drive by. The driver knew he had slowed down too quickly.

"What will you do?" the passenger asked the driver in broken English with a Russian accent.

"I slam on brakes; make him crash," was the answer.

Brian depressed the gas pedal slowly and cautiously to get a closer look at what was sticking out. Suddenly the brake lights came on, and smoke came from the tires as they screeched on the pavement. Fortunately for Brian, the police package on the Ford Expedition didn't only increase the performance of the engine; it also increased the size of the brakes. Brian hit the brakes, narrowly missing the box truck. The truck sped back up and continued speeding up.

The driver knew what he had to do. Getting arrested was not an option. There was a gun in the truck just for this purpose. He pulled out the sawed off, double barrel shotgun. The passenger looked at him and nodded, and closed his eyes.

"This is Sergeant O'Niel of the Maine State Police. I have a white box truck with Maine plates. Delta Echo Bravo Foxtrot..." As he was making his radio call for backup, the truck swerved to the left, hit the guardrail, and rolled onto its passenger side. It slid for a while before coming to a stop. Brian already had his lights going, stopped a car length away from the vehicle. His Glock model 20 was in hand, and pointed at the driver side door of the truck. Expecting someone to pop out, he crept slowly and carefully around the front of the truck to look in through the windshield. The driver had a gun in his hand but lay lifeless on top of the passenger. There didn't seem to be any faces. As he got closer, the situation became clearer.

Given the skull fragments and brain matter all over the passenger window and the driver's side roof, it was evident what had happened. The driver had killed his passenger, then shot himself. This only added to the many questions running through the Sergeant's mind. He decided to walk to the back of the truck to investigate what he had seen earlier, hoping he was wrong. The lift gate of the box truck opened further when the truck tipped over, its contents now halfway out of the truck. The rolled up clear plastic with a human arm poking out of it looked like something from a movie scene. He checked for a pulse, but there wasn't one. He knew at this point that the best thing to do was to keep his hands off everything so as not to tarnish the crime scene. He called it in on the radio and shortly after, other officers started showing up. Lights were set up; they blocked off the highway, setting up a detour. The crime scene van pulled in and started taking pictures of the area and all the evidence. They slowly and methodically unrolled the body in the plastic. One investigator removed the wallet from a pocket to find an FBI badge and identification.

Carla Rand woke up to the sound of her phone ringing. "Agent Rand," she answered. Her lips and fingertips went numb. Any cop or federal agent hated to hear one of their own dying on the job. This was close to home. There were not many FBI agents assigned to Maine. That's why she had gotten the call. If an agent was murdered in New England, all federal agents in the area were called in. All they had told her was an FBI Agent had been beaten to death and found in a truck on 95 North. She knew Dan had gone to Portland yesterday and was supposed to be back before their date last night. She took a deep breath. "Get a hold of yourself. Don't jump to conclusions." It didn't work. She quickly got dressed and grabbed her gear.

The scene was packed with several law enforcement branches. One of their brethren was dead, and from the looks, he didn't go easy. Carla recognized Dan's supervisor as she walked up onto the scene. As soon as he saw her, he started towards her. The look on his face told her all she needed to know. He reached out and put his hand on her shoulder. She heard his words, and it shook her to the core. She stayed strong on the outside, but she was crushed. She nodded as he spoke, but didn't really understand anything he was saying. She glanced past his shoulder to see body bags that were obviously occupied. Dan's supervisor followed her eyes. "He is in the one closest to us." He didn't have to tell her not to unzip the bag. She walked over to him and put her hand down on the cold black bag. "Oh Dan… who did this to you?" she paused to hold back her emotions. "I will get them, Dan. I will nail their sorry asses to the wall."

Anne looked out the window of the restaurant out towards the water. The sunrise was bathing the water in an amber light, while a seagull was calling in the distance. Normally, a scene like this would make her smile and feel warm, but her concern was growing more and more for Russell's cough. She decided she would call Dr. Long's office herself on Monday morning. She was prepping food for the upcoming day when she saw Melissa walk in. She looked to be beaming. She had a punch to her step, and she was humming a tune as she came into the restaurant.

"Hello, Anne."

"Hi Melissa, you seem to be very happy this morning."

"Yes…yes, I am. Um. I have a lot to say, and I am not really sure of the order I should say it."

"Well, just start talking and let it all out." Anne already had an idea where this was going.

"I am pregnant. I asked Jack to marry me. He said yes," Melissa blurted out almost as one sentence.

Fortunately, there was a chair behind Anne where she plopped down on, mouth open, trying to formulate a response. Melissa was obviously happy, and Anne didn't want to be the person to rain on her parade. All she could think of is how fast Jack and Melissa's relationship had gone up to this point, but that love was strong, and true love knew no timeline.

"Congratulations!" Anne said, getting off the stool and giving Melissa a hug. "Did I hear you right, that you asked Jack to marry you?"

"Yes, I wanted to be the one who would ask. I wanted to break the tradition and all stereotypes a bit. I had already planned to ask him. The pregnancy is just a bonus."

"How far along are you?"

"I took a home test a couple weeks ago and another one yesterday morning. I am going to see an OBGYN soon to make sure. Jack is going to go with me. Only you and Jack know right now, and I want to keep it that way for a while."

Anne gave her another hug. "I won't tell Russell, but I wouldn't be surprised if Jack doesn't go talk to him. This is one of those times a man needs to talk to his father. I do have to say you and Jack certainly have...unconventional ways."

That last sentence hit Melissa with an edge. Was Anne really happy about this? It was certainly far from traditional, and the Finns were a traditional family with their Sunday morning breakfasts and all. They were also pretty open-minded. She decided not to read too much into it. She was happy and didn't want to spoil it.

"Are you hoping for a boy or a girl?" Anne asked to stop the awkward pause.

"I don't really know. I just want a healthy baby."

"What do you think Jack wants?"

"I don't know that either. He seems pretty protective of Lizzy but, at the same time, very big brother-like to Josh. He was pretty happy when I told him I was pregnant. He keeps saying, 'I'm going to be a father.' I had to remind him about the husband part."

"About that.... do you have a date in mind? Any plans?"

"I don't know, I probably won't start to show until June or July.... Wait... We could do it on the day we met! One year from the day he fished me out of the water!" Melissa said while beaming. "We could do it right on his boat! Right at the very spot. A small gathering of just close friends and family."

"That sounds like a great idea. We could do the reception at The Harbor."

"That could work. I just have to find a way to keep the media out. Even though they don't stalk me as much as they used to, the news of me getting married is sure to dig up some hype."

"I guess you never really retire from Hollywood. How is everything going with the... big change?"

"My estate is completely liquidated and disbursed to different charities, including the Russell Finn Foundation. I have set up a little rainy-day fund for me and Jack, and now I will set up a trust for the next little Finn. I have already started volunteering at the school. Originally, I did not plan to start taking classes myself until the fall, but I have started taking some online courses to get my teaching degree. As soon as that is done, I will be Boothbay Region High School's drama and music teacher."

"You know you will get the job?"

"Well, I work cheap, and you know one of those charities I donated to," Melissa said with a wink. "Mrs. Niles says I still have to prove myself to her and the school board."

"I have no doubt you will do great. I am very proud of you, as always. I am not going to lie, I wish you and Jack would slow down a bit, but I am happy you are happy with him, and he is happy with you. I can't wait to hold my grandchild. Melissa, you are going to be a wonderful mother, and I will be here for you whenever you need me." She thought about warning her about how hard pregnancy can be, mentally and physically, but there would be time for that. "What are your plans for today?"

"I wanted to see if you needed some help here so I could get some more hours in?"

"Definitely, we're doing a taco night tonight, and I could use some help cutting up the vegetables."

Jack was walking down the hill to the family dock in Lobster Cove. He had fond memories of this hill and this cove that he would soon be sharing with his own child. He remembered getting off the bus, tossing his bag on the porch, then running down this hill to get into his boat, the first Red At Night, then taking off for a boat ride, or striper fishing. Soon, another generation of Finns would enjoy it. His reminiscence was broken by the sound of his father coughing. It had gotten worse lately. As he got closer, he could see his father hunched over the empty lobster tank in his boat. Jack ran as fast as he could. When his feet hit the dock and made a thundering noise, Russell looked up to seek Jack with a concerned look on his face. He could see Jack was about to say something.

"Don't you start. Your mother was on my case last night. It is just a cough," Russell barked.

"Just a cough, my ass; I see that blood at the bottom of the tank!"

Russell looked at the blood swirling around amongst the water and various shells and seaweed at the bottom of the tank. He could taste its vile taste even over his strong black coffee. He had lost friends to lung cancer. He knew how it started and how it almost always ended.

"Don't you worry, Jack; I am going to see ole' Dr. Long real soon."

"You better, old man.... You're going to be a grandfather real soon!"

The sickening feeling that had been haunting Russell lifted, and he felt like he was hovering. This was something he had wanted for so long. Being a father was great. Especially to kids like Jack and Lucy, but to be able to see the next generation of his bloodline and spoil the hell out of them. Parents had to discipline the kids. Not Grampy's and Grammy's, no, they could wind up the little tikes then pass them right back. Russell couldn't help but break into one of his dancing and singing fits.

"We are having a baby, my baby and me, we are having a baby, my baby and me!" He sang while prancing around the *Old Smoke*.

"You ain't having a baby. I... Melissa is having a baby! She also asked me to marry her, and I said yes!"

Russell stopped his dancing only to give more energy to the grin on his face. "That girl doesn't do anything normal. Ha ha ha!"

"You are not supposed to know about the pregnant part, girl stuff. She is going to talk to mom about it, but I didn't quite get permission to talk to you about it."

"Oh, I know. They like to keep it a secret for a while just to be sure.... Your mother and I waited three months before we made the big announcement. I will keep it a secret. Thanks for telling me."

"Well, it's a lot happening in a very little time. Kind of crazy when you think about it. We have been a whirlwind since the day I fished her out of the water. I have to say I get worried we are moving too damned fast, but at the same time everything seems to be going well."

"Jack, some things just happen that way. No different than finding a hot spot in six fathoms of water in January. All logic says the lobsters should be in deep water offshore, but it happens. Enjoy what you have, my boy. Life is too short not to."

Jack took a moment to soak in the advice, and another to process the cryptic ending. Russell stepped out of the boat and embraced his son.

"Congratulations, boy. I am proud of you. You and Melissa are going to be great parents. You two are going to have a wonderful life together, I just know it."

Carla sat on the bumper of her car watching the crime scene get processed. She didn't move a muscle; just watched as everybody worked until all the bodies were gone and the box truck had been taken away. Dan's supervisor had offered to get her a ride, but she declined it. She stood up and took a long breath. "I have work to do," she said to herself out loud. She was startled by her phone ringing. It was Commissioner Stryker. She hit the screen to take the call.

"Carla, where are you? Are you safe?"

"Yes, but Dan is...." Stryker cut her off.

"Dan is dead, isn't he? Carla, I don't know what is going on. I missed a call from Dan last night and just got around to listening to it this morning. You are in danger. Where are you now?"

"On the side of 95, but headed to my office."

"Good, I will meet you there; you are armed, right?"

"Always, one on my hip, another on my ankle, and I still have that crazy arm knife thing that Michael Williams gave me."

"Ok, kid. Head on a swivel."

Carla put her phone back in her pocket. "Just what in the hell is going on here?" she asked herself. It was the start of a jigsaw puzzle, but all the pieces were scattered all over the place, and she knew she didn't have them all. She got in her car and started sorting things out. Dan was in Portland yesterday to finish up his retirement paperwork. He was supposed to meet her in Boothbay Harbor for their date. Instead, he had called Commissioner Stryker, and he wound up dead in a box truck. The truck was driven by two unknowns, and one of them shot the other before shooting himself; or, at least, that was what the investigators at the scene thought had happened. The border of the puzzle was starting to form. Her gut was telling her something, her head just needed to back it up with facts.

Chapter 2

Demetri Balfour was sitting in his Portland apartment watching the news when the story came on about the overturned truck on the northbound side of 95. The reporter talked about a distinguished FBI agent had recently brought down a Russian drug and gun operation. He was found beat to death at the scene. The authorities made no comments other than that when the police Sargeant first attempted to pull the truck over, the driver shot the passenger then took his own life. The license plates on the truck were fake, and there is no record of the driver or his passenger. Demetri Balfour, a normally calm and collected individual, slammed his fist on his oak desk. He was hoping to have Carla Rand in his possession in a couple days, if not less. She was getting close to uncovering his operation, and he was running out of people and time. He looked down at his desk to find a newspaper article about an Oscar winning actress's early retirement. "Aah" he said to himself. "Maybe, Ms. Rand, you need some motivation to stop pursuing me." He rubbed his chin while a devilish grin slowly appeared on his face. "Paul, bring my car around," he shouted to a subordinate outside the door. A plan was forming in his head, but he needed the right weapon.

Commissioner Stryker parked his truck and walked to the DEA branch office located on the 3rd floor in an office building. He sat down in a chair in the waiting room, a typical uncomfortable government issue chair. The building was quiet since it was the weekend; just a few people milling around; none asked him if he needed help. It was awkward and pleasing at the same time. He really wasn't in the mood to answer questions, and didn't feel like small talk. Carla came through the door, walking fast and looking like hell. Eyes puffy and red, face showing all the signs of being under strain. Even though he could see she was upset, she still walked like she was on a mission. She motioned for him to follow her, and he almost had to jog to keep up. She pulled some keys out and unlocked her office door, and opened it.

"So, what have you got?" she asked as they walked into her office.

"Before I play this voicemail, I am going to warn you. You can hear everything that is happening to Dan. These are his last moments, and you hear every detail. Somehow in the.... action, his phone must have called me, like a pocket dial," he said while she closed the door to her office behind them.

"Ok." Carla took a deep breath to prepare herself and sat down at her desk. "Play it."

Commissioner Stryker put the phone on speaker and set it on her desk. You could hear loud thuds, the almost hollow sound of petting a dog on its rib cage, but louder and every so often, the crack of bone. After a few hits, the sound of Dan gargling on his blood while trying to breathe. The thuds stopped after what felt like an eternity, then silence. After a moment, a familiar voice could be heard. The voice was muffled, no doubt by the blood that was surely covering the cell phone.

"Wrap him up in plastic and put him in a truck. We can be in Boothbay Harbor -------------- When he is found, they will ID him, and Agent Rand will definitely be notified. --------------------- more batting practice or whatever you two want to do with her for fun."

Rand slowly tipped back in her seat. She had no idea what to feel. She had just listened to a brother officer of the law, a friend and mentor, and what she had hoped to be more, get beat to death. Not only that, but her life was also now in danger. There were a few more words spoken and some background noises she couldn't figure out, then the voicemail stopped. Commissioner Stryker removed the phone from her desk. He sent the voice mail to Carla's phone, then looked up at her. She was staring out her window now. Blank expression on her face.

"What is your next move?" he asked, not knowing what else to ask.

"Monday, I will run this up the chain of command, both DEA and FBI. I am going to continue to work the Balfour case."

⁂

"Don't you think you should back off? They are coming for you now."

"Let them come.... I hope they come. There is something much bigger here than drugs and guns." She pulled some photos out of a file from a drawer in her desk. "Look at these. These were taken from that yacht we seized the night we took down Tommy and the Russians."

"I thought FSB took that and all your evidence."

"Not FSB... Balfour had men posing as FSB. They even had Dan fooled, surprisingly. I noticed while the yacht was at the Coast Guard station that nobody was going on and off. No investigation at all. I even checked with Brian Blethen, the station chief. Nobody going on and off. Also, he didn't know anything about it being transferred over to FSB; he thought ATF and FBI still had possession of it. So, I went over Dan's head...way over. I called the Russian Embassy in DC. They had no information about the FSB being here or conducting an investigation. So, I went back onboard and started taking pictures and looking around. Especially around the fuel tanks. When I went onboard the morning after we got her, I noticed one tank was showing empty on the gauge. I had Michael Williams go with me. Figuring he was a diesel mechanic, he may be able to help. Funny, it was his past life in the military that helped more. He said a lot of big yachts like this would use fuel tanks as storage for guns, drugs, or cash. We found a hidden hatch that led into a fuel tank that had been converted into a storage space. It was huge. Big enough for me and Mike to crawl around in." Out of the same drawer, she pulled the photos from, came a small plastic bag with a piece of cloth in it. She tossed it on top of the photos. "I found that stuck to one of the hinges on the hatch."

"Holy shit, Carla, is this leading to where I think it is?"

"I don't know, Commissioner; it's a leap, but my gut is telling me it is. Unfortunately, no DNA or anything was found on that piece of cloth. I am not even certain its clothing. It could be anything. Just my gut."

"Did Dan know any of this?"

"No, I was going to tell him last night, but..." Carla looked down at her desk, holding in the emotions weighing on her.

"Well, first thing you need to do is get yourself some protection. This Balfour guy is one scary man. He already killed Dan, and you are in his sights next."

"I know. I am always carrying at least two firearms and this crazy knife thing Michael gave me." She flicked her wrist, and a small black knife shot out from her shirt sleeve. "Did you know he used to be special ops in the Navy? It never even showed up on our background checks. He told me he was Swick... SWCC."

"Yeah, he and Lizzy go to the gun club a lot and shoot. The guy is a surgeon with a Glock 20. 100yrds away and his group is the size of a basketball, and he complains he used to be better."

"Good to know. Listen... I am going back to my apartment just to get some things. After that, I am going to come back here, switch cars, and stay in a hotel for the weekend. Other than following up on what just happened, I am going to lie low. I have told you things that you are not technically supposed to know. Guess what... I am going to continue to do so. I don't know who I can or can't trust here, in the ATF or the FBI, but I know I can trust you."

Commissioner Stryker gave her an assuring nod and walked out.

The Finn Family Sunday breakfast started as usual. During the colder months, Russell and Anne had plastic panels up on the screened in porch, turning it into a sunroom of sorts. A couple of large folding tables, along with every chair from all three houses on the compound, gave plenty of room and seating for everyone. The guys were all in the garage admiring the 57 Chevy that Melissa had gotten Russell for Christmas. Russell couldn't wait to drive it around town with Anne. They had been coming out and sitting in it some evenings. The snow was still hanging around a bit, not strange for March in Maine. The conversation circled around the car, then the boat racing season, lobster price, and other town affairs. The conversation in the kitchen was much the same. Melissa had moved up from pancake duty to the sausage gravy and biscuits cook. Though there was no real rank structure in the kitchen, as you gained experience in the kitchen, Anne would challenge the girls. Anne had actually dropped back to pancakes, allowing Lucy to take over the eggs. The Williams family was over this morning as well, so Liz and Abigail helped out with coffee and toast.

"Gosh, Mom, if this family gets any bigger, we will have to start doing these breakfasts at The Harbor."

"Family's grow, Lucy. It's what makes them so special." Anne said while shooting a subtle grin to Melissa. Melissa saw the grin, and her cheeks got warm and red. Everyone else in the kitchen hadn't seen it except for Elizabeth. Soon everybody was sitting at the table, enjoying breakfast. To Melissa, there was nothing better than this moment right here. All week long, she waited for Sunday morning breakfast. She loved the time in the kitchen getting the meal ready. Then sitting together, talking about the week and what had happened. It felt so good to her to be around people that genuinely cared for each other and for her. After everyone had their fill, except Jack, Michael, and Josh, who seemed to never get full,Russell started the traditional highs and lows for the week. Melissa reached under the table and gave Jack's hand a squeeze. Jack turned to her and smiled, and gave a little nod. Melissa returned the nod. It became Melissa's turn to speak.

"My low for the week was learning just how much stuff people took care of for me without me even knowing. I never had to worry about paying bills. My accountant took care of that for me. Sounds silly, but it has been an adjustment. My high for the week is." She paused for a breath and looked to Jack, who took the que and stood up as well. "I asked Jack to marry me, and he said yes!"

The table applauded at the news, and congratulations were given. The happy couple sat back down, still holding hands.

"Wait a minute, you asked him to marry you? Ain't that kinda backwards?" Michael asked.

"Not in this age, Dad. Melissa is a modern woman. Strong and independent." Elizabeth stated.

"Lizzy, I know that, but what is wrong with sticking with tradition?"

"Dad, human sacrifice used to be a tradition. The man being the bread winner while the woman stayed home used to be the tradition. You can look at lots of traditions that have stopped or evolved with time. Women are allowed to go into combat now."

The table got quiet, and everybody became spectators of this debate between father and teenage daughter.

"I am all for women's rights, Elizabeth, and don't forget, I served with those women in combat, but what about tradition? Some things need to remain sacred. Look at what we do here. You girls make the breakfast right. It's a tradition."

"And you men go in and clean my kitchen!" Anne chimed in. "Now you go back in time a bit, and that would never have happened. We cook for you, not out of tradition. We cook for you because we like to cook. WE enjoy that time together. Bonding, passing on our knowledge to the next generation of women. Much like you guys do out here. Now I am a 5th generation Maine woman. I am about as old school and traditional as it gets. I will tell you something right now. If that old ox over there hadn't have asked for my hand when he did, I would have taken his at the end of a shotgun and dragged him to the church."

"I have no doubt about that." said Russell. "She was dropping hints as subtle as cinder blocks before I asked. What is everyone up to today?"

"Dad and I are going to the gun club and do some shooting. A little range therapy!" said Lizzy.

"What? Lizzy, you shoot guns?" Melissa asked.

"I have been shooting since I was 12. It has always been dad's and mine... thing. A little bonding time."

"I suppose you are one of those anti-gun people like the rest of Hollywood." Michael said.

Melissa paused a bit. Michael was still so stubborn and ignorant with his stereotype of Hollywood. She wanted to lash out. "No, I have never shot a gun, but I have always wanted to try."

Michael thought for a second. He glanced at Lizzy and could read her face. Shooting was always his and her time to share, but she thought the world of Melissa. "How about you go with us. You can shoot Lizzy's old 22."

"No, I couldn't impose your father daughter time, Michael."

"Really,Melissa, I mean it. We will come pick you up. You should learn how to shoot. You don't have a driver or bodyguards anymore, and you never know about some crazed fan stalking you. Not to mention, there is a reason we call it Range Therapy".

"Ok, I am in! You guys can pick me up here, then. Do I need to bring anything?"

"No, but though we shoot for fun, we take it seriously. When we get there, Lizzy will go over the range rules and general firearm safety. You need to listen carefully."

Melissa nodded her head in agreement.

The men got up from the table and started clearing the plates, doing dishes, and cleaning up the kitchen. Jack was on washing duty, washing the pots and pans that didn't go in the dishwasher. Josh brought in the plates, silverware, and other items from the table. Sam loaded the dishwasher while Michael dried off the pots and pans. Russell sat and watched.

"I am not saying it's wrong; I am saying it's odd to have a woman asking a man to marry him... her... whatever. Are you going to take her last name too?" Michael asked.

"No, she is anxious to be a Finn. I technically asked her first. I think it is less about independence and more about her being humble." Jack replied.

"How has the media been since she got back?" asked Sam.

"That comes and goes. We see reporters here and there taking pictures of us at random places. I am sure they will be all over the place as more details of the wedding come out."

The women sat at the table overlooking Lobster Cove. They watched the water in the cove ripple with the gentle breeze while talking about wedding and reception details. Melissa explained that she wanted the ceremony to take place on Jack's boat out in Linekin Bay, right where he pulled her out of the water. Not only would it make it a symbolic moment, but it would help keep the media away. After the ceremony, they would cruise back to The Harbor for the reception. That would be a much bigger event with some of Melissa's Hollywood friends along with the Finn's friends and family. They started laughing at the thought of the two different factions of people. The guys came filing out of the kitchen and joined in the talk about the wedding. Sam caught a look from Lucy. He knew she wanted to get married. She had been dropping hints since they moved in together. He actually had the ring in his pocket. He was just waiting to ask for Russell's permission first. Now, with Jack and Melissa, he didn't know what to do. Should he wait a bit? He didn't want to take away from their moment, but he and Lucy had known each other longer and had been living together. He didn't want it to seem like he was asking because of Jack and Melissa, either.

The Williams said their goodbyes and told Melissa they would be back to pick her up after dropping off Abigail and Josh and getting the shooting gear. Russell picked up the Boothbay Register and sat to read while Jack and Melissa went to sit on Jack's porch.

"Do you want a boy or girl, Jack? Melissa asked while sitting down on Jack's porch overlooking Lobster Cove.

"Both! I want fraternal twins! If you give me a boy, we'll get busy making another baby and keep going until we get a girl. I don't care if we end up with 10 boys or ten girls just to have at least one of each."

"Are you nuts!"

"No... well, maybe a little. I have been very fortunate to be an uncle to Lizzy and Josh. Both have their merits and hardships. I want to walk my daughter down the aisle. I want to teach my son how to be a good man. I want both worlds. I want to sit and watch you braiding our daughter's hair for her first day at school. I want to watch you get our son ready for his first date." Jack was pacing back and forth on the deck while taking sips of coffee. Melissa could see the sheer joy in his face. "Then, Melissa, I want to sit right here on this porch and watch our grandkids running around on the lawn."

"Jack, you're getting a little ahead of yourself, don't you think?"

"Oh, I know I am. I just can't help thinking about the future, our future."

Melissa stood up and walked to Jack. She wrapped her arms around him and gave him a kiss. She leaned back against the porch railing and looked up into Jack's face.

"How long do you think we have before Michael and Lizzy come to pick me up?"

Jack could tell by Melissa's grin what she was thinking. "We could have a quicky." They grinned at each other for a moment before heading into the house. "Jack!" They heard, outside just as they started into the bedroom.

"Yes Mom?" Jack said back as he recognized the voice.

Anne stepped onto the porch. "Jack, I need to talk to you about something if you have a second."

Jack rolled his eyes at Melissa and started walking back towards the door. "Whatcha need, Mom?"

"Can we go for a walk?"

Jack paused for a minute. If his mother wanted to go for a walk, that meant she wanted to talk. More than likely, it would be about Melissa being pregnant and the wedding. He also knew that when Anne Finn wanted to talk, you had better oblige. He grabbed his coat and went to the door.

Jack and Anne started their walk out of the driveway and around Apalachee Pond. The Finn family had been taking walks "up around the pond" since they first settled in Lobster Cove. Sometimes it was just a way to burn up some time. Often, it was a time to have a serious talk.

"Jack, I am worried about your father."

This caught Jack by surprise; he thought that this was going to be about him and Melissa. "What are you worried about, Mom?" he asked back, already knowing what was on her mind.

"His coughing, his lack of energy, he is sick, and I know it's not a cold or the flu."

"He coughed up blood yesterday when I was talking to him. He said he is going to see Dr. Long soon."

"Oh, I hope he does. Hell, if he doesn't, I am going to knock him out and drag him there myself."

"Melissa and I will keep a close eye on him. Everything will be ok, Mom."

Anne smiled back at Jack. She knew he was as worried as she was, but didn't want to panic his mother. She decided to change the subject.

"So, going to be a dad yourself soon, huh?"

"I knew she was going to tell you. Thanks for being there for her."

"Jack, I love Melissa; she is a great woman. I am glad you two found each other.... I do wish that you guys would slow down. I mean, you two haven't known each other for a year yet. Now you are getting married and have a baby on the way."

"Mom, me and Melissa are meant to be together. That I am 100% sure of."

Anne wanted to ask how he could be so sure. In the grand scheme of things, they really hadn't put their love to the test. They hadn't had to figure out what bill to pay and which one they would kick back another month. They hadn't lived together to learn each other's bad habits. She smiled a bit, remembering her and Russell getting acclimated to each other many, many years ago. She shifted her train of thought. Jack and Melissa did have something special. She saw it the first time she saw them together.

"I know you two will be fine. Just remember, marriage is work. Work on both sides. When you two start living together, it's fun in the beginning, but there will be times you two will drive each other crazy. As for you guys being parents, I have no doubts you will raise a wonderful child and be great parents. Melissa has some instincts that she doesn't even know she has, despite no bond with her mother. I saw it when she held that baby and how she handles her younger fans. You are not so bad yourself the way you have always looked after Lizzy and Josh."

"Thanks Mom. I am pretty anxious to be a dad. I hope she and I will be as good as you and Dad.

"You will be better; I am sure of it."

Melissa had decided to visit Russell while waiting for Michael and Lizzy. She saw Russell was slowly rocking in his rocking chair on the porch, reading the Boothbay Register and puffing away on his pipe. As she walked through the door, he glanced up over the paper.

"Hollywood, you going shooting in a bit, ain't ya!"

"Sure, what are you doing with the rest of your day?"

"I am going to go down to the dock house and start building a crib."

"A crib?"

"Yes, a crib for painting buoys. What kind of crib do you think I mean?" He said this with a grin, and his pipe gently clinched in his teeth.

"Russell Finn. I may not be the saltiest sternperson in Maine, but I know there is no such thing as a crib for buoys. I also know that son of yours just had to talk to you."

Russell sat up in his chair a bit, put the paper down, and took his pipe out of his mouth. His cheeky grin grew to a big smile.

"Congratulations Hollywood."

She took a step closer to Russell and he got up from his chair. She wrapped her arms around him in a big hug.

"I am going to be a mother, Russell."

"And a damn good one, I imagine."

She relaxed her arms and took a step back. The old man's eyes were watery, and a single tear started forming in the corner of his right eye.

"I'm going to be an official member of the Finn family too."

"Oh, you're already an official member, but I will be some proud to see you with the Finn name. You are going to take our name?"

"Yes definitely. I may be partly feminist, but I will be proud to carry the Finn name."

At that time, Michael and Lizzy were pulling into the driveway. Melissa gave Russell a peck on the cheek and then got in the truck. Russell waved at them as they drove out of the driveway. After a short drive on typical Boothbay wavy roads, they were outside of the gate at the Boothbay Region Fish and Game Club. Lizzy hopped out and unlocked the gate, and Michael drove in. As soon as the truck was past the gate, Lizzy locked the gate again and got back into the truck. They drove a few hundred yards to a small cabin with a sign saying, "Club House". Across from the clubhouse was something that looked like a covered porch but with no house attached. It had several benches at waist level, then some more sitting benches. Michael and Lizzy grabbed a couple of plastic boxes that looked similar to toolboxes. They placed them up on the waist high benches.

"Alright, Lizzy, give our guest here a run down on weapon safety. Start with the 3 basic rules."

"First rule is to treat every weapon as if it is loaded. Second, don't point the weapon at anything you don't intend to shoot. Third, keep your finger straight and off the trigger until you intend to fire. Now there is a fourth one, but it doesn't apply to all our guns. Keep the safety on until you intend to fire. Only the Beretta 9mm has a safety. Now, if someone is down range, all weapons stay sitting on the bench. Hands off! If you have a misfire or something goes wrong, put your hand up, and Dad or I will come help you. Always keep the muzzle pointed down at the ground or down range. No turning around while you have a weapon in your hand."

Melissa was slightly nervous now, but all the rules made sense. She was taken back a bit by how serious Lizzy was about it. She was usually so bubbly. "Ok, I got it."

Michael was back from setting up the targets. "Melissa, I set yours up at 5 yards. That's where I started at. That's where Lizzy started at. Lizzy will show you what sight picture is and how to aim. When she says clear to shoot, fire 5 rounds nice and slow. Don't worry if you are not hitting the bullseye. We will get you there."

Lizzy held up one of the guns and explained it was a Glock 44, and it shot a 22 round. She showed Melissa the sights and how to line them up on the target. With the gun still unloaded, she had Melissa hold the gun up like she was going to shoot and pull the trigger.

"You ready?" Lizzy asked.

"Yes," Melissa answered.

Lizzy inserted a magazine into the gun, pulled the slide back, then released. Melissa thought it looked like it did in the movies. Lizzy put the weapon on the bench and told Melissa to put her ear plugs in, and Lizzy did the same. She then nodded to Melissa to pick it up. Melissa picked it up and lined up the sight. Lizzy said, "clear to shoot." Melissa placed her finger on the trigger and slowly pulled it back. The pop startled Melissa, and the gun shook in her hand; she took a deep breath in through her nose and caught the smell of gun powder. Now that the first shot was over, she squeezed the trigger four more times, concentrating more on keeping the gun steady and on target. As Lizzy instructed, she placed the gun back on the bench with the muzzle pointing down range.

"Good job. Looks like all your rounds went low and left. That means you're doing one of two things or both. You're anticipating the recoil and squeezing the grip while you squeeze the trigger. Both are common with first time shooters. You have 5 more shots left; try to relax a bit. Take deep breaths. Dad and I are going to shoot now as well."

Melissa picked up the gun again and took a deep breath. She paid special attention not to squeeze the grip while she pulled the trigger. She fired the next five shots much slower than her first. She could hear Lizzy and Michael shooting beside her. It actually helped knowing they were not watching her. After she fired the last shot, the slide stayed back. She placed the gun on the bench to watch Lizzy and Michael. Lizzy's target was set at 25 yards. Far enough so Melissa couldn't really see where she was hitting, but soon enough, there was a golf ball sized hole in the bullseye of the target. Michael's target was set at 50 yards. His gun made a much louder noise than Lizzy's or the one she was using. Just like Lizzy, a golf ball sized hole formed on the bullseye.

"Wow, you guys are good. Lizzy, you obviously learned from your dad, but Michael, where did you learn to shoot like that?"

"U.S. Navy."

"But I thought you were a mechanic in the Navy."

"I was, I was a mechanic and boat driver for Seal Team 4."

"You were a Navy Seal!"

"No, no, no. I was what they call swick. S.W.C.C. We supported Seal Team 4 down in Central and South America. Insertion and extraction by water. We had to have weapons training."

"Well, thank you for your service."

"You're welcome. It was a privilege."

Melissa got better and better. Eventually she had a group the size of a grapefruit, so Lizzy moved her target out to 10 yards. After a couple hours of shooting, they decided to wrap it up. The raw March cold air was starting to sink in, and Melissa's arms were getting tired. While Lizzy went to retrieve the targets, Melissa talked to Michael.

"Michael, thanks for letting me come. I know this is usually you and Lizzy's time, but I really appreciate bringing me along."

"No problem; Lizzy thinks the world of you. I think she respects you more now than she ever did when you were a star. You are doing some good things up at that school too. Lizzy's friends talk about you all the time. Girls need a positive role model outside of the household. I had you pegged all wrong from the start."

"Oh, that's water under the bridge. You were being protective of your daughter and your best friend. I can respect that."

"Hey, while I got you here, I do have a favor to ask. Lizzy has a picture of you in a dress from some movie... It's from the Judy Garland one. What is the chance you still have that?"

"I know the picture you're talking about. She had me sign it. Unfortunately, I don't have that. I think the studio kept that; why?"

"She has prom coming up in a few months. I wanted to surprise her with it."

"I will make a few calls, but I can't promise anything."

"That's fine. The prom isn't until May."

"Planning ahead a bit, huh."

"Yeah. I am kind of going all out. Getting her and her friends a limo too."

"Wow, a limo. You are going over the top."

"Strategy, my dear... strategy. I get the limo reserved now, and if a boy asks her to prom, they will ride in the limo. To the prom, and straight back home after the prom. Rather than riding around with some hormonally driven teenage boy. Also, if I rent the limo, Josh gets to ride in it too. Now I have eyes in the limo."

"Ha ha ha. You have that all thought out, don't you?"

"Hey, I was a teenage boy myself once. I know what goes through their mind. You were a teenager once. Don't you remember?

"No prom for me. Private schools and tutors. No school sports, no dances. I did get to travel a lot to different places."

"You know, in the past, I have jabbed at you for playing the "poor little rich girl," but I get it. I have been able to watch my kids play sports, make friends, go to sleepovers and such. I did much the same. I can't imagine not growing up like that."

"You know, Michael, if there was one thing, I really wish I could have experienced being taken to prom. It just seems like a rite of passage."

Michael pondered that thought for a bit, then Lizzy walked up to them. They packed away all the weapons and ammo and got into the truck. After dropping Melissa off at Jack's house, Michael turned to Lizzy and spoke.

"I got an idea."

Chapter 3

At 9:00 AM Monday morning, Carla Rand was at the Maine State Police's Portland garage looking at the truck from the crime scene. She could see the damage from turning over on to its side, and as she walked around, the acrid smell of blood and flesh pierced her senses. The shattered windshield and the headliner of the truck were covered in blood, brain matter, and fragments of skull and other bone. She remembered Dan's supervisor saying something about how the driver and passenger had no faces left to identify and that their fingertips had been mutilated beyond identification. It was no surprise to her that the crime scene investigators had worked over the weekend. An agent down meant all hands-on deck, and nobody complained. Beside the truck, there were tables of evidence found in the truck. She saw the bloody sawed-off double barrel shot gun the driver had used to mask their identity. Then she saw something familiar; in an evidence bag, there was a small piece of cloth, like the one she found on the Russian yacht. If she didn't know any better, it looked like it came from the same source. Unfortunately, she didn't have the other piece with her. She wasn't sure of handing it over to the people handling this case. Who could she trust? Could she just follow her gut instinct that the two pieces of cloth were a match? If they were, what did that mean? The yacht and this truck had something in common. Someone or thing had been in this truck and in the yacht. Whatever it was, someone wanted it hidden. She turned to investigate the back of the truck. There was dried blood on the edge of the tailgate. Dan's blood, no doubt.

"Can I help you?" A voice startled Agent Rand. She turned to see an older woman standing there wearing a lab coat with an FBI badge clipped to it. She had gray and white hair tied up in a bun and large frame glasses. Carla could tell she wasn't happy with her presence here.

"Hello, I am agent Carla Rand with the DEA. I am here just checking in on the investigation." Carla said while showing her badge.

"DEA? I wasn't aware that DEA was involved in this. I was told it was strictly an FBI investigation."

"The agent that died, he was a good friend of mine. I was just hoping to get some answers."

"Well, Miss Rand, here at the FBI, we don't go poking around evidence in an active investigation. You shouldn't even be in this room!"

Carla knew she was right, and she needed to keep a low profile. She didn't even mean to be seen. "You are right, my apologies." She started to walk away when, on the evidence table, she saw some bloody zip ties. She remembered Dan's hands were not restrained. "Ma'am', may I ask where these zip ties came from." The lady rolled her eyes, and at first looked like she was going to tell Carla that it was none of her business. The lady took a breath and said, "They were all over the inside of the truck. Today, everything is being sent out for DNA analysis. Here is the number of the agent in charge of the investigation. Call him if you have any more questions." She paused a bit and looked at Carla with a slight hint of compassion. "I am sorry about your friend." Carla took the card and walked out of the garage. Her next stop was the Maine State Prison in Warren, Maine.

Tommy Macintyre sat in his cell, reading a book. He had adjusted to his new life, but he still hated it. Commissioner Stryker had got him a subscription to the *Boothbay Register*, but he couldn't bear to read it. Boothbay Harbor was moving along without him. The Finns had improved his old business. All he had now were memories, and those haunted him. He relived that night that he had taken Stephanie's life over and over. He could have just gone to the police, and he might have gotten some time for dealing drugs, but now he was here for life. This cell, this prison, was the rest of his life. The same schedule every day, the same bland food, the same shower scene. He trembled at the thought. He didn't even fight it anymore. He just let them do what they were going to do. Eventually, they would move on to someone else. He cried every night, to himself and quietly. He was startled by a knock on his cell door.

"Macintyre, you have a visitor."

Tommy was puzzled. He had no family. His only friend in the world died that night he was arrested. Shot in the head by that Russian bitch. From what he had heard, she had got what she deserved. The warden had a tight grip on Tommy's arm; he couldn't understand why, he was handcuffed, in a prison. Where was he going to run off to? The sounds of this place were maddening, the constant steel doors being opened and shut, yelling of prisoners and wardens. The warden opened the door to the visiting area, and at a far table he saw Agent Rand; he thought it was odd she was seeing him here and not in one of the official rooms. He walked with the warden until they got to the table. Tommy sat down and decided to speak first.

"You come here to gloat?"

"No, Tommy, I am here to find out if you can remember anything else. A name, a place, anything."

"I told you and that Ross guy everything I knew. I had never even met that Balfour dude."

"When Katiya and Cashmere first approached you, did they tell you they were jumping over anybody. Bypassing someone."

"They never mentioned anybody, but anybody that knows the drug business knows you're supposed to use someone in Portland. I never heard of the guy. The Russians pulled me aside and offered me a bunch of money to allow one of their trucks to come up here from Boston. At first, it was supposed to be just drugs. Then they started doing guns. I knew I was in way over my head." Tommy stopped for a second and looked around for a bit. Carla could tell he was coming around to a thought of some sort. "You know... I think those Russians got in over their heads too."

"What makes you say that, Tommy?"

"I don't think they realized just who they were dealing with. For five years, we bypassed the dealer in Portland, that Balfour dude. That's a long time to get away with that, and for the volume we were moving, now even the CIA is looking for this Balfour guy."

"What.... CIA? Did the CIA come talk to you?" Carla asked in a state of confusion.

"Yeah, but it was weird; he seemed more interested in Jack's Hollywood chick than Balfour. He asked me if Balfour was going to go after Melissa or Balfour knew who Melissa was. I told the guy I never got a chance to talk to Balfour. He met here like you are, not in one of the private rooms police and lawyers usually use."

"What did he look like? What was his name, Tommy?"

"He said he had a cold, so he was wearing a mask, but I never heard him cough. He had a black ball hat on and shady glasses. Not sunglasses, but tinted. He said his name was Smith, Agent Smith."

"Well ,Tommy, I won't waste any more of your time."

"Funny."

She gave a nod to the warden, and on her way out of the prison, asked to see the visitor log. Any other time, she would have laughed, but not today. Listed there for visiting Tommy was a John Smith, and he was listed as a friend. The CIA wasn't looking for Balfour, but someone else was, and his name sure enough wasn't John Smith. She asked to see the camera footage, but it was useless. Not only was the video grainy, but the hat, mask, and glasses blocked his face. All she had was another piece of the puzzle that didn't seem to fit.

Demetri Balfour sat in the back seat of his car, watching the activity at The Harbor. Agent Ross never told him any of the background information on how they had arrested Tommy, Katiya and Casmiere Ornikoff. He did mention a blonde girl that was informing Agent Rand about what was happening at Tommy's. After seeing all the recent news about how the famous Melissa Andrews was dating someone in Boothbay Harbor,she was working on a lobster boat and was now working here at this place where all this had unfolded. It only made sense to him that she had discovered something, and she was talking to Agent Rand. "Melissa Andrews and Agent Carla Rand, Oh Agent Rand, I bet you would tell me everything I need to know if I had you, and your little friend." Balfour said to himself. A sly grin stretched across his face; rather than torture and interrogate them, why not sell them. He had already been selling people. Transporting them in his yacht and in his trucks. "What a price a retired actress would bring in." He looked at the photo he had of Agent Rand; "She would get a good price, too." He put the photo away. This idea that was formulating could solve his problems and make him a lot of money. It would have to be an overseas buyer. Normally, he would contact a broker, but this was too big. He would keep surveillance on this, Melissa Andrews, and Agent Rand. His mind kept working on how to make it work. This was much bigger than the others he had grabbed and sold off. People knew these two; if they disappeared, people would look for them. They would have to be shipped overseas so nobody would ever find them again. He watched Melissa walk outside to put a bag of trash in the dumpster. His eyes narrowed as he focused on her. Much like a predator leering at its prey.

"Paul, I want to keep an eye on her. She and that Agent Rand. They will pay for meddling in my affairs. For now, let's go back to Portland; we are going to need some help, and I need to make some phone calls."

"Yes, sir," Paul said as he put the car into gear and drove away.

~~♦~~♦~~♦~~

Russell was sipping his mug of coffee and looking over some paperwork when he heard a call over the VHF radio.

"The Harbah, you there, Russell" the radio sounded. It sounded like one of his fishermen, Don "Old Mud" Sproul.

"Yeah, Old Mud, right here. Whatcha need?"

"I just found old man Townsend dead on his boat. I saw the boat not moving, and his dog was barking. I came along side and saw him on the deck. I checked for a pulse but got nothing. I have already called the Coast Guard. They are going to take care of him, but asked if someone was available to bring the boat in and take care of the dog."

Russell's heart sank. He had been friends with Zeke Townsend for a long time. "I will grab Hollywood and shoot out there." He took a second. "You got something to put over him?"

"Yes, Russell, we put a blanket over him."

Russell went over to the kitchen where Anne and Melissa were working.

"Hollywood, put a coat on and grab some bacon. Meet me down to the boat. We have to go get.... We have something to do."

Anne instinctively put some bacon in a plastic bag and passed it to Melissa. She could tell by Russell's expression this was not a time for questions. Melissa put her coat on but looked at Anne, confused. Anne gave her a nod as to say, "Just go with it."

Melissa heard the *Old Smoke* start up. She broke into a jog when she did. As she turned to go down the ramp, she saw Russell untie the boat. He certainly was in a rush.

"What's going on, Russell?" She asked while jumping into the boat.

"You know old man Townsend, has a boat named *Patricia Lynn*?"

"Yes, he is a sweet old man. Has that dog, Jarvis, always with him."

"Don Sproul just found him in his boat. He passed away."

"Oh, Russell, I am so sorry."

"Coast Guard is on its way out to bring him in. I am going to run his boat in. The bacon is for the dog. Jarvis is usually very friendly, but he may get a little defensive given the circumstances. I gotta find someone that will take care of Jarvis for a while. Ole Zeke has no local family. He lost Patricia three years ago. They have one kid, but she moved to London."

Melissa remembered how Jarvis would always run up to her, wagging his tail. She would often pet him while Zeke and Russell talked. One thing she missed out on growing up was having a pet.

"Russell, I will take Jarvis until Zeke's family figures things out. I am sure they will have enough to worry about."

"I don't know how long you will be stuck with him. Could be as much as a week or more."

"That is fine, Russell. It's what we Finns do right?"

Despite what was going on, Russell smiled at Melissa. He nodded in approval as he pushed the throttle ahead. There was a light fog this morning, but not so much you couldn't see where you were going. It was enough to make everything feel wet and cold. Like winter's bond wasn't ready to let go yet. The kind of day that locals would call "raw". He could see Don and Zeke's boat just past Tumbler Island. Off to starboard the Coast Guard patrol boat closing in. Before he could reach his radio to talk to them, they called him.

"Fishing Vessel *Old Smoke*, this is the United States Coast Guard. We plan on approaching the port side of the fishing vessel *Patricia Lynn*."

"Ok, we will come up alongside the starboard side. Don, you can untie yourself and head out. We got it from here."

"Sounds good, Russell. Jarvis seems pretty upset. Right now, he is lying down beside Zeke with his head on Zeke's chest. He let me check his pulse and put the blanket on him, but he knows me from the dock. I am sure you will be fine, but not sure how he will do with a…. strangers."

Russell looked over at the patrol boat getting closer.

"Hey, Coast Guard, why don't you hold up a second and let us get there first. I know you have a job to do, but I think it would be easier if the dog wasn't there. Jarvis is a friendly dog and all, but your guys may spook him a bit."

"Copy that."

Russell brought *Old Smoke* alongside. He intentionally kept the visor of his hat down so as not to look at his old friend. He wanted to get the boat tied up and gain composure before looking. To his surprise, Melissa was already stepping over the rail into Zeke's boat. Russell looked on, and she crouched down and approached the dog.

Melissa could see Zeke's hand sticking out from the blanket Don had put on him. It was her first time seeing a dead body so close, and it shook her nerves. She had talked to the man that hand belonged to just last week. Jarvis was lying down with his head on Zeke's chest, just as Don had said. The dog didn't even seem to acknowledge she was there. "Hey Jarvis," she said in a low, soothing voice, offering her hand to be smelled by the dog. Jarvis raised his head slightly and pawed at his owner's body as some way to indicate that something was wrong. "I know Jarvis; he is gone. I need you to come with me, buddy." Jarvis didn't move; he just burrowed his head into the side of the lifeless body. Melissa got closer, fearing that the dead body would just jump up and startle her, but she knew that was unreasonable. She started petting the dog's head. Jarvis seemed to ease his tension. A slight whimper emerged from the dog. As if he now understood what was happening, as Melissa petted him, she could feel how cold he was. She slowly got even closer and started moving her hands then arms underneath the poor dog. She slowly picked up the dog and pulled him close to her. He gave her a quick lick to the face then nuzzled his head under her chin.

"Guess we didn't need the bacon." Russell said.

Melissa slowly got back on-board Russell's boat. He made a bed out of some hoodies and rain gear he had. She slowly eased Jarvis down onto the bed and got out the bacon. Jarvis just lay there, looking over to Zeke.

"Ok, Hollywood, you sit here with him, and I will untie the boat. Let yourself drift away a bit before you try to get going. I will catch up with you back at The Harbor."

Melissa sat there, petting Jarvis while feeding him pieces of bacon. She gave Russell a nod to acknowledge him. Russell untied the boats and gave *Old Smoke* a push with his leg. The boats slowly separated. Jarvis sat up in his makeshift bed and let out one last howl. It was a goodbye to his friend, father, and master. Melissa got choked up a bit watching this dog's loyalty, even in death.

Jarvis was dark brown, with traces of black around his mouth, eyes, ears, and tail. Zeke had gotten him as a puppy from an animal refuge in Westbrook, shortly after losing his wife, to help keep him company. Jarvis was built for that purpose, it seemed. Always a happy dog but also very smart and obedient, most of the time. Wherever you saw Zeke, Jarvis was not far behind. At the dock, Jarvis had a habit of greeting people. He would jump out of the truck and walk around to people, as if he was saying hi. Jarvis had become a fixture at the dock. Melissa always took time to pet him, and he would give snuggles in return. Now she looked into his almond eyes that almost seemed water filled. She put the *Old Smoke* in gear and started heading to The Harbor. She glanced back at Russell and the Coast Guard boat; they were taking Zeke on to the patrol boat now. Russell would be along shortly. She could see him making calls on his cell phone. No doubt trying to get in touch with his family. She looked down at Jarvis, who had coiled himself up into a ball with his nose tucked under his tail.

"Don't you worry, Jarvis. I am going to take good care of you."

Before long, she and Russell were tying up the boats at The Harbor. Police Chief Nick Upham was there, waiting on the dock.

"Ms. Andrews, I talked to Mr. Townsend's family in London; they are ok with you holding on to Jarvis for a bit, until they figure out who can take him permanently. I went into his house and got you his dog food, bed, leash, and some of his toys. I also grabbed a blanket from Mr. Townsend's bed. I figured it would make Jarvis feel more at home."

"Nick, I told you to call me Melissa. No matter if on duty or not. What do you mean, take him permanently? They don't want him?"

"No, where they live, they don't allow pets. They seemed very disinterested in having one."

"What will happen to him?"

"Probably back to a kennel for adoption."

"Never mind that. I will keep him."

Russell had just walked up but had heard most of the conversation, "You sure, Hollywood?"

"Yeah Russell. I got this. Come on, Jarvis."

Jarvis popped his head up in a confused fashion. Then slowly got up and walked over to Melissa. He followed Melissa to her Blazer and hopped in on command. Melissa helped Nick unload Jarvis's things out of the cruiser and into the SUV."

"If you change your mind, I can come pick him up."

"Ok, but I think we will be fine."

Melissa got into her Blazer and closed the door. Jarvis was sitting upright in the passenger seat, looking at Melissa. Russell walked up to the driver's side window, and she rolled it down.

"I think I am going to start calling you Full Throttle instead of Hollywood. You certainly charge right into things. Have you ever had a dog?"

"Nope, has Jack ever had a dog?"

"Nope, I don't know why we never had one. Just never thought of it, I guess."

"Well, he... we have one now. I am going to take him home and get him settled in."

"Thanks for your help and taking care of Jarvis. I am sure Zeke would be happy."

Russell walked away, and Melissa called Jack. She knew he was busy helping Michael haul his boat, but she felt this shouldn't wait. After filling him in on the news of Zeke, Melissa brought up Jarvis.

"So, I agreed to take Jarvis."

"For how long?"

"Umm for good?"

"OK.... um.... so, you have a dog now?"

"Yes... WE, have a dog now."

"Well... ok... umm."

"Jack, I know this is something people usually talk about, but we both know Jarvis. I couldn't stand the thought of him being taken back to the shelter. Jack I am sorry I didn't talk with you first, but....."

Jack cut Melissa off. "No apologies needed. So, we have a dog now. I can take him lobstering with me, or he can hang out with you at The Harbor. You did the right thing, Melissa."

"Love you, Jack. See you later."

"Love you too."

Michael was driving his truck and overheard the conversation.

"Got a dog now huh?"

"Yes, Zeke Townsend died, and his family didn't want Jarvis. So, Melissa adopted him."

"Wow... You guys are trucking right along and checking all the boxes. Getting married, getting a dog, next thing you will be telling me is she is pregnant."

Jack had to work at keeping his face straight.

"Yeah, we said we would take things slow right from the beginning; boy, ain't we friggin that up." He continued to talk to change the subject. "So why are you hauling your boat all the way up to your house when you have a nice shop right there next to the water?"

"Can you keep a secret?"

"Yeah"

"I am having the Lowell brothers work their magic on the hull. I am having them put a hard chine on her and reshape the keel to make it more hydrodynamic. This thing will be as slippery as a bar of soap when they are done."

"Ah ha Lowell's huh? Nothing like boat knowledge that dates to the beginning of the lobster boat."

"They are going to design everything, then Jody Merton will do all the glass work. I will pop in and out here and there, but I am still wrapping up a few winter projects. It also helps keep the project top secret."

"Yeah, when I haul out *Red At Night*, I only have some minor stuff to do. Have you go over the engine with whatever it needs. Paint the bottom. I should only be in your shop for a week or so."

Michael paused a bit. There was something he had been meaning to talk to Jack about but didn't know how to bring it up.

"Jack... how is your father doing?"

Jack took a deep breath and exhaled slowly. "I think he is sick. I don't know what, but he has got something."

"I saw him coughing so hard he had to sit down the other day. I rushed over to check on him, but he said he was just fighting a cold."

"Same here; keeps telling me there is nothing to worry about."

Michael could see concern on Jack's face and decided to change the subject.

"You and Melissa set a date yet?"

"June tenth, one year to the day I pulled her from the water. We talked about it last night and have a basic plan down. A "welcome dinner" Friday night. The ceremony will take place on my boat with the wedding party. Yours and dad's tied up alongside for other guests. We figure that will help keep unwanted media away. Then we all cruise into The Harbor for the reception. She is inviting Chris, RDJ, Taylor, and Jim Sterling."

"I can't get over how you can just throw those names out like they are normal people."

"Because they are normal people, they just have abnormal jobs. Anyway, that reminds me. I need to ask you something."

"Well, it sounds like you need to ask for my boat, and the answer is obviously yes."

"Yeah, that, and will you be my best man?"

The question hung for a moment in the air, Michael had not expected that, he knew he should have.

"Of course. I would be honored to." He said, with a growing smile. "Who is going to be her maid of honor?"

"She is going to ask Lizzy. She figured my mom would want to sit and watch. That, and Mom is more like a mother than a friend to her. She is going to ask Abigail to be a bridesmaid, and we want Josh to be an usher."

"Christ, you are recruiting my whole family! Who will give her away?"

"She is going to ask my dad to."

"Oh, Russell will love that."

"Yeah, he will be proud as a peacock."

They pulled the boat up to Michael's driveway. Jack got out and helped him guide the boat into his shop. Michael had already lined the inside of his shop with plastic to keep the fiberglass dust from getting all over the shop and had rigged up a few fans for air circulation. They unhooked the trailer from the truck and shut the doors. Michael made a pot of coffee, and the two friends sat and talked a while.

It was about lunch time when Jack went to see Jarvis at Melissa's house. When he walked through the door, Jarvis had stood on guard and let out a small growl; Jack put his hand out and gave Jarvis a calm "Easy boy." Jarvis turned broadside to Jack and leaned on him a bit.

"There you go, ole' boy. No reason to bark at me. I am a good guy." Jack said, while petting and scratching the dog.

"Oh, I see how it is. Now the dog is going to get all the attention instead of me." Melissa said, sarcastically.

"Don't blame me, you brought him here. How are you doing? Kinda of a dramatic day."

"They had Zeke covered up by the time we got there. I could see his hand sticking out from the blanket, it was sort of scary and sad all at the same time. I have never seen a body before. Jarvis was lying next to him. It took some smooth talking and some bacon to get him on your dad's boat. I am glad I was there to help. It was the first time I ever ran *Old Smoke*

"Well, his family will come, and there will be a funeral. We will do a boat parade too."

"Boat parade?"

"Yeah, all the area fishermen will line up. Usually with the deceased's boat taking the lead. Followed by family and best friends. We do a big circle around the harbor. If the loved ones are on the dock, we swing in close to pay our respects."

"That's great. You guys and your traditions. It must be amazing to watch."

"It's a sight for sure. Brings us together a bit. Speaking of together... what are we going to do? Technically, we are engaged, right? So, we should probably start thinking of living together."

"I had been thinking about that for a while now, like before I asked you to marry me. Even before I knew I was pregnant. What would you think of moving in here with me?"

Jack stood there, dismayed for a moment. He had never considered leaving the family compound. "Why here? Why not my place?"

"Jack, I love your family and your house, but I want a little more privacy. I just bought this place, and it was my first move towards this new life... except for dating you."

"Well... I don't know... never thought about this part. I just assumed you would live with me. I was already planning on turning my office into the baby's room. I have a shop and the dock house to work in. I am not saying no, but I need to think about this. I don't know what my mom and dad will think."

"Jack, we can put a nice big garage in here. I was already thinking about doing that anyway. As far as your mom and dad... you are 30 years old, right; most men don't live one hundred feet from their parents."

"I know Melissa, but you know how dad has been sick lately. I want to be close by if something happens."

"I have noticed your father not being well, and I understand you are concerned, but what are you going to do if something does happen? Call 911? Your mom is going to do that. It's less than five minutes to your parents' house. Look, we have some time to think about this and talk more, but I want us to live here."

"Ok, I am going to head home and get some buoys painted in the dock house. That will give me some time to think about this some more. Love you." He said, as he leaned forward and kissed her.

"Love you too," said Melissa as he stepped away, tension still in the room.

Chapter 4

Agent Rand was sitting in her office again, looking through the case files and trying to find something new. Something she hadn't seen before, anything. But it was all the same. Same evidence, same statements. She looked out of her window at the city. "Portland," she said aloud. It was almost perfect. Portland was big enough to do business in, but such a small city in such a rural state that nobody would consider major crimes happening here. The drugs and guns that sent shockwaves through the state just a few months ago were already forgotten about. Life went on. She knew there was still something going on, and she feared she knew what it was. She had no substantial proof, just small pieces, figuratively and literally. One small piece of cloth was in her possession, and another at Dan's crime scene. "Dan," she said aloud, again talking to the nothingness of her office. He may have known something, and that got him killed. She was sure the FBI was probably dissecting his house right now. If not, they already had, and the place was sealed off and under surveillance. A trigger went off in her head. Dan's house would definitely be under surveillance, and not just by the FBI. Whoever killed Dan may be watching the house as well. Waiting for the FBI to leave, watching to see if they found anything. She had a plan now. She would drive by Dan's house to scout it out, try to see someone watching the FBI. She grabbed the keys to the unmarked car she was using instead of her own and started toward the door.

At the door stood a six-foot, four-inch wall of a man. Blue jeans and a black hoodie with no logo on it. Red hair and a goatee, no smile, and icy blue eyes that almost looked white. He took up the entire doorway. She could see the impression of a firearm under his hoodie on his right hip. He was twirling keys with a big BMW key fob in his right hand. She was scared. How did this man get up here? Was this the John Smith that had visited Tommy? Fortunately, his gun was covered by his hoodie, and with keys in his right hand, she could have her weapon out and pointed at his head before his would clear the holster. She decided to go for it, get the upper hand, then ask questions. Just like thousands upon thousands of times in training, she unholstered her Glock 19 and brought it up so the sight was lined up on the man's forehead. Her finger was straight and off the trigger,but if he made a motion towards his firearm, it would go to the trigger with a verbal warning.

"Who are you?" Agent Rand said, from clenched teeth.

The man seemed completely unphased by the gun pointed at his head. He slowly walked a couple steps into the room, then sat down in a chair by the door. "You already have my card. Someone at the Maine State Police's garage already gave you that, or at least that is what I was told." He spoke with a southern draw that annoyed Rand.

"If you are FBI, where is your badge?" She asked, lowering her weapon but still at the ready.

"I don't make a habit of reaching for things when someone wants to toss me a 9MM luger round at 1400 feet per second. I am not into piercings, certainly when they involve my cranium."

"Cut the shit talk and show me your badge now!" she demanded.

"Ok, ok, darling. Don't forget now you were the one snooping around my investigation. Why are you so wound up any way" The man pulled a chain from his neck, and out came a leather wallet with an FBI I.D. and shield. Rand looked at it. It looked real enough. His name was Andrew Roberts.

"Did you know Dan, Agent Roberts?"

"Danny, hell, yes, he was my training officer for a while."

"What kind of coffee did he drink?"

"That damn blueberry coffee. Friggin year round too. Me, I like the pumpkin spice stuff in the fall, but stick with the regular stuff the rest of the year."

"How old are Dan's kids?"

"No kids, ma'am. Ole Danny boy was never even married."

"What was his girlfriend's name?"

"Well... given the text messages I have read on his phone, his girlfriend's name was going to be Carla, as in Carla Rand, as in DEA Agent Carla Rand, which brings me to why I am here. I am the one supposed to ask the questions. You are supposed to answer them. So far, you have threatened a federal officer. Now I hate to arrest you, so put that gun away, sit down, and let me start asking the questions."

Carla Rand holstered her weapon. This agent passed the sniff test; now, to see what he wanted. She took a step back and sat in her chair. She placed her arms on her desk to look less threatened and defensive. "What questions do you have for me?"

"Well, I don't like to dance around and work up to a grand finale, nope. I like to slap my cards hard on the table, like I am holding a royal flush. So let me start by asking, just what were you and Ole Danny boy planning to do with all that money?"

"Money?" Carla tipped forward in her chair and cocked her head as if to hear Agent Roberts better. "What money? What the hell are you talking about? What do you mean, what we were going to do with it?"

Agent Roberts stood up and took out his cell phone, and turned the screen towards Rand. In a duffel bag were stacks of $100 bills. He swiped to another picture, and that showed a toilet with the tank cover removed with more money in a clear plastic bag. He swiped again to find a desk top computer with cash stuck inside.

He swiped again and again, every time a new hiding place with stacks of $100's. He swiped one last time, and she saw what looked like a bookshelf, but it swung away from the wall, like on hinges. Behind it, the drywall removed, stacked between the studs were bundles of cash.

"That one there is my favorite, kind of James Bond like. He had just opened a crypto currency account and was making regular deposits. He had quite the little system going, buying crypto with cash, little bits at a time. Yet his checking account looks completely normal, yours too."

"Mine too? You checked my account?"

"Yep, as soon as I saw how friendly you guys were getting on your texts together, then saw all the money, I investigated you. You guys were both in a great position for our Mr. Balfour to use. You two were the only ones to see the FSB folks, but they were not FSB, were they. You made that little fact well known after they had already escaped. Then you put a stop to all the drugs and guns going to Russia. I bet ole Demetri Balfour wasn't happy with that. I think you guys decided to cut poor old Demetri out of the deal. Get the guns and drugs out of evidence and sell them yourselves. Demetri didn't like that idea, so he found Dan, and he is looking for you. Which is why you greeted me with your Glock."

Carla Rand was a mix of anger, confusion, and heartbreak. Agent Robert's southern accent, mixed with his smug demeanor, made her want to punch him in his face. Her chest was heavy, and her throat felt hard and constricted. She needed to gain traction. She needed time to think without this southern bumpkin and his annoying accent.

"So, if this is what you think, why aren't you arresting me?"

"Oh, I will; I most certainly will. I just need to wrap this case up a little tighter. You need to have your ducks in a row with a case like this. Not to mention, you are still the small fish in this case. I don't mind letting you swim around a bit, see if the bigger fish comes for you. That works two ways too. Maybe you start thinking about how they dealt with your boyfriend, and you start getting scared. Pretty soon, a confession starts looking real good. I am sure jail time would be better than batting practice."

"Nice, use me for bait, or I confess to something I didn't do."

"Pretty clever... guess who taught me that. Ole Agent Dan Ross, back when he was a loyal servant of justice, not turn coat for a human trafficking drug lord."

"Get the fuck out of my office!" She yelled, finally losing her composure. The emotions, lack of sleep, had finally found the end of her rope. Agent Roberts wrapped his big hands around the arms of the chair rather awkwardly and stood up slowly. He looked her dead in the eyes while standing up, like he was trying to force words from his stare, and walked out of her office. She got up, slammed the door hard, and locked the door. She paused for a bit, thinking about those last couple of seconds. She kneeled down on the floor and looked up at the arm rests of the chair. Sure enough, a bug. "What the hell is going on here?" she thought to herself. First, this Agent Roberts mentioned the human trafficking, then makes it obvious he is planting the bug. Then she started thinking about the pictures she had seen of Dan's house and all the money hidden all over the place. She thought about crypto and knew what it meant. Crypto was virtually untraceable, and able to be converted into real currency, any currency, anywhere. Dan was planning on leaving. He had fooled her. She stood there, zoned out, staring at the lamp on her desk. "What to do, what to do?" she asked herself.

Agent Roberts got back into his car, turned on his earpiece, and put it in his ear. He hoped she figured out what he did. He wasn't certain if Balfour had another guy in the FBI or not. He didn't know if Dan was involved with the human trafficking or not. His gut told him he could trust Carla Rand. He started to hear her voice in the earpiece.

"Commissioner Stryker?" He heard Agent Rand say.

"I need to talk to you, A.S.A.P!"

"That is fine, Boothbay Harbor sounds good about now."

"OK. I will meet you there."

He could only hear one side of the conversation, but he heard enough. He knew who Stryker was. He had been on Agent Ross's tail since Balfour enlisted him. He had just started watching Balfour and starting an investigation when Dan Ross fell in his lap. He couldn't believe it at first, he knew Dan. Like he told Rand, Dan was his training officer and helped him get started. Dan was a damn good agent, too. At first, he thought he and Dan had accidentally overlapped. He backed off because he didn't want to blow Dan's cover. That was when the big take-down happened on the night of the 4th of July. Agent Roberts felt a big relief at first, then the jail break happened. At first, it made no sense at all. To storm a prison, assassinate two suspects, not kill a single guard. What better way not to attract too much attention. Nobody would really care about two Russian thugs, especially if they had a hand in killing a local girl. Agent Roberts walked into Dan's office that morning to ask him about the case and to give him what he had on Balfour. Dan was out of his office, so he figured he would leave the file on his desk. Dan's personal laptop was open to a real estate page, all the houses were in warm tropical locations. None in the US. He had known Dan for a while. Dan loved Maine. He had gone on about retiring up north. Buying a cabin on Long Lake up in St. Agatha. Dan had always told him, "You see a loose thread, you pull it, no matter what."

He didn't know if Balfour had reached out to Ross or if it was the other way around. He had his suspicions that Ross tracked down Balfour. Dan Ross had been driving a desk for years. Then suddenly, he gets a phone call from the Maine Marine Patrol Commissioner about two Russians using a lobster business to move cocaine, and he was back in the field again. It was almost genius. Get paid by Balfour, nail the Russians, and have your name on one of the biggest drug busts the state had ever seen. Good way to retire. Statements from Ross and staff at the prison said that Ross had gone in and had the Ornikoffs and Balfour all put in separate interrogation rooms. Ross probably texted Balfour's men what rooms they were in, and how many guards, and where. Ross made sure to be outside with Rand when the hit and jail break took place to distance himself. Then he escorted the fake FSB guys to the yacht and signed paperwork releasing all the drugs and money. He had no doubt that had all been planned way ahead of time. It was a good plan... well, until Agent Rand kept pulling at any loose thread she could find. She had the drugs and guns recalled before they left, much to Balfour's dismay. So much that he had killed Agent Ross.

Agent Andy Roberts shook his head at the thought. Since he had been watching Balfour, six people had been killed. Dale Rines, the Ornikoffs, and now Dan Ross, plus the two thugs in the truck. He didn't care, they were scum, and Dan was the worst of all. His boss, on the other hand, did care and was not happy. It wasn't like he just stood by and let people die. Dale happened so suddenly, and the case as a whole was much bigger than one small time drug dealer. The Ornikoffs being killed and Balfour escaping certainly did not help. When Rand had discovered about the fake FSB guys and had stopped the transfer of the guns, drugs, and cash, he felt that Dan and Carla were in danger. Balfour was a pro, though, like a shadow. Hard to follow, and with his stunt at the jail, some people thought he was some type of vigilante and really didn't put too much effort into finding him. Dan's death had no hard evidence leading him to Balfour. The two thugs in the truck had no readable fingerprints, no faces due to the shotgun blasts, and no DNA on file. All he had was his gut, telling him that this was Balfour.

The recent visit with Agent Rand told him a lot. "She knows something." he said to himself. "She thinks she is in danger." His thought process kept spinning. The way she pulled that gun and was slow to re-holster it. "Hopefully I have earned her trust enough for her to let me in the loop." His thought process kept spinning. This case had been a balancing act of knowing when to step in and when to watch. Roberts had a feeling something big was going on here, and if he had jumped in, he would have lost his chance to see the big picture. He was willing to lose a few drug dealers and a turncoat agent if he could bring down a bigger operation. He was not going to let anything happen to Rand or any other innocent person. He kept Agent Rand's car in sight and followed her to Boothbay Harbor.

Commissioner Stryker was sitting in a booth seat at The Harbor when Carla Rand walked in; not far behind her was a large red headed man in a black hoodie. Carla sat down and slid to the inside of the booth. Agent Andy Roberts sat down next to her; before he could plant his butt on the seat, Agent Rand started in.

"Ok, no games, just what the fuck was going on in my office?" She had said it louder than she had wanted. A few people turned their attention to them.

"Now there you go again, you need to settle down a bit. Kinda rude, don't you think, not introducing me to your friend here."

"Agent Roberts, this is Department of Marine Resources Commissioner Jed Stryker. Commissioner, this is FBI Special Agent Andrew Roberts. Now can you tell me what the hell that was all about in my office?"

Agent Roberts held a finger up to Agent Rand to tell her to wait a moment. He could see her getting angrier by the gesture. He turned his head to the Commissioner. "Commissioner Styker, you were the one that got Ole Danny Boy involved in all of this mess, wasn't you. Why was that?"

The Commissioner looked annoyed at first, he took a sip of his coffee and drew a breath. "I also brought Carla here in on it too. She wasn't getting the help she needed from the DEA; I had known Danny from a long time ago. I knew he was pulling mostly desk duty, but I figured he would rattle some cages at the bureau, and the bureau would rattle the DEA. I was surprised when Danny said he would come down and take a look himself."

"Dan was dirty." Rand blurted out.

Agent Roberts looked at the Commissioner, measuring the look on his face.

"What? Dan Ross dirty? No way, no way in hell."

"You didn't know?" Roberts asked in an accusing tone. He watched the Commissioner's face change from genuine surprise to absolute contempt.

"Let's you and me get this straight right now. I know being the Commissioner of DMR may not amount to much as compared to the DEA or FBI. But you will respect me, and if you are going to accuse me of being dirty, you better have some fucking proof to back it up."

Carla Rand looked on as the two men stared at each other. She had watched Commissioner Stryker punch Tommy. He could hit, but Andy Roberts was a mountain.

"Look." The Commissioner broke the silence. I knew Dan for a long time. Whenever he needed something on the water, he came to me. If he needed to know about the fishing industry, he came to me. For the past couple years, he would talk to me about retiring to northern Maine. Now, I had been watching Tommy MacIntyre for a while, had my guys go down there and poke around, but as Marine Patrol officers, their scope was limited. We had no probable cause. Then Tommy reported that Russell and Jack Finn had been selling shorts. I called the DEA first because I figured the FBI was too busy to play a hunch. When Carla arrived, I had her put on a patrolman uniform. I had also gotten a call from Russell Finn who had heard about Tommy reporting Jack and Russell. Now I kept Tommy busy down at the dock while Agent Rand here started looking around. She managed to bug Tommy's phone; Lizzy, who worked for Tommy, told Agent Rand about the shipping receipts not adding up. We listened to a conversation between Dale Rines and Tommy, and something was off. So, we planned to watch them. That is when I called Dan in."

"So, Ole Danny Boy sees this drug deal going down. He knows enough to know that Tommy and the Ornikoffs are bypassing a major player. So, he decides to rat out Tommy and the Russians to Balfour and help the FBI and DEA set up one of the biggest drug busts in New England. He gets money from Balfour and a big pat on the back from the justice department. Then he plans to run out of the country." Agent Roberts continued with the events.

"But he didn't factor me in. He was counting on me backing off and letting the fake FSB handle it." Agent Rand explained.

"Yeah, he didn't count on you pulling on the loose thread. His own advice came back to bite him." Agent Roberts added.

"I think it's time for Roberts here to hear the voicemail, Commissioner."

Commissioner Stryker pulled out his phone and played the voicemail. The table was somber for a moment.

"Now they are coming after you." Agent Roberts said while looking at Agent Rand.

"So, can we go to the FBI?" asked Commissioner Stryker.

"No, they think Carla is involved. I think Balfour has someone else in the FBI. I don't know where, and I have no proof. Just my gut."

"Your gut is good enough for me. There is also another player. I went to visit Tommy in prison. I asked if he could add anything else. He really didn't have much to add other than he had been visited by a CIA Agent by the name of Smith. I checked the visitor log, and it showed a John Smith as a relative. He was wearing a mask, glasses, and a hat, so, no visual." Agent Rand added.

"This case is a fuck of clusters! Thugs with no ID, a dirty FBI Agent, another possible FBI agent tipping off Balfour, now we have a mystery man that may or may not be a CIA Agent…and we have to keep all of this between us because we don't know who we can trust." Commissioner Stryker said, incredulously.

"What we need is a man on the inside for us, and I think I have an idea."

Russell had just gotten off the phone with Dr. Long and was zoned out, looking out the window. Dr. Long was adamant about Russell coming in the next day for an appointment. The tone in the doctor's voice was what worried him. Serious and concerned, none of the usual banter that Russell was used to. The warning that he may send him up to Portland for a "closer look" scared him more. Now he was second guessing himself. Why had he waited so long? Why didn't he call the doctor the first time he coughed up blood? He knew why. That wasn't the way he was taught. "Be tough," his father preached to him. His father once had Russell drill a hole in his fingernail to relieve a blood blister underneath it from hitting it with a hammer. Russell remembered him "sanitizing" it with some homemade whiskey and a lighter. How that man lasted as long as he did, Russell could never figure out. With Zeke's passing, his own mortality was coming into question. How much time did he have left? Would he see his kids get married? Would he see his grandchildren? He closed his eyes so tightly, it squeezed a single tear that ran down his cheek.

"You Okay, Russell?" asked Anne, standing in the office doorway of The Harbor. For a moment, Russell contemplated telling his wife he was fine, but the weight of his thoughts was too much. He walked over to her and held her.

"I am not ready to leave yet, Anne. There is so much more I want to do and see. I am scared, Anne." Russell said as he held his wife. Anne just stood there, holding her husband. Fearing the worst and hoping she was wrong.

"We don't know anything yet, Russell. Don't get yourself upset yet. It could be something simple, and if it isn't, we will deal with it. I was about to go to the house for a bit. Are you okay, or maybe get someone to take over for you?"

"Yeah, I will find myself some work to do and get my mind off this." Russell said as he let go of Anne. He felt a little better talking about it, but the weight of his mortality was still there.

Anne walked away with her own weight. There was much more to say, but this wasn't the time. "What would I do without Russell?" she thought as she got in her car. Russell was the only man she had ever loved. In their 33 years of marriage, they had been through many tough times, but never this, never any health issues. She took a deep breath and exhaled slowly, trying to exhale the pressure and all the bad feelings. "Don't jump to conclusions, girl. Be strong."

Jack arrived at his house and walked down to the dock house; as he entered, he looked around the old dock house which was more like a walk-in time capsule. The walls were open studded, and there was no insulation and had splatters of his father's buoy paint. They were decorated with old signs from past businesses in the area and Boothbay Register articles that had been cut out and stuck between studs. Random nails on studs where drying buoys would soon hang. The wood stove where countless old oak trap runners had met their fate and kept the place warm. The same old lobster crate where his father had sat him down to give him…the talk. In the not-so-distant future, he may be giving the same talk. The old coffee maker that you could measure the amount of coffee it had brewed over the years in gallons. The 60's era pale green fridge with chrome trim and handle, and a dent in the door that Jack didn't know how it got there. Yet, the old fridge could still keep beer ice cold. The dock house had a blended smell of the ocean and burning wood that added to the coziness.

While painting buoys in the dock house, Jack thought about the idea of moving to Melissa's even more, and the more he thought about it, the more it made sense to him. Family compounds were a thing of the past, and even though his parents never invaded his privacy, there were times it was awkward. Way back when Stephanie would spend the night and he would see his mother the next morning trying to pretend she didn't know Stephanie had spent the night. His parents knew anytime Melissa spent the night. He loved his house, but he was ready for change. Melissa's house came with quite a bit of property, if he remembered right. It was all trees, but he could put a shop in pretty easily. They might even have to add to her house anyway. It only had one bedroom, and that was a loft. What would he do with his house? He would have to rent it out. That property could never leave the Finn name. How would his parents feel about a stranger living so close? His dad wouldn't care. He loved people. His mother, on the other hand,... she would have her reservations. She was the one that would take convincing. He kept on painting buoys, and listening to the radio, and thinking about his soon-to-be wife and child.

After painting for long enough the radio was repeating some of the same songs, he decided he had done enough for one day. As he was cleaning up, the door opened, and his mother walked in.

"Hi, Mom. Glad you're here. I need to tell you something," said Jack, while cleaning off his paintbrush.

Anne, not really in the mood to talk about anything serious, was hoping for some lighthearted talk with her son. Maybe ask about baby names or plans for the wedding, but when her son needed her, she was always there. "OK, Jack, what is on your mind?"

"Mom, I am thinking about moving in with Melissa. I know we have the family compound thing, but I am about to start my own family, and I want a little space. Now I will still come and....." Anne cut Jack off mid-sentence.

"I think that is a great idea. Yes, you can still come and mow the grass and plow in the winter. What will you do with your house?"

"Um... what... wait..." Jack stammered a bit. Shocked, his mother agreed with the idea. Confused, she completed his thoughts on the mowing and plowing and was already jumping to the "what to do with the house?" question. "I think I will rent it out. Actually, I know I will. I want to keep that property in the Finn name."

"I can help you find a good tenant if you don't mind?"

"Sure, I am surprised you are okay with this. Out of you and dad, I figured you wouldn't be a fan of the idea."

"Jack, like you said, you and Melissa are about to start a family. You need room to grow, make mistakes, and have some privacy. Your walls are thinner than you think." Anne paused a bit while Jack blushed and turned away from his mother. "I know I may show concern with how fast you and Melissa are going, but I am happy for you both and proud of you both. I can't wait to hold my grandchild."

"Thanks, Mom," said Jack, as he gave his mother a hug.

Russell was finishing fixing the dock cleats when he saw Melissa walking Jarvis on the leash. If there was anyone that could brighten his day, it was her. There were only a few times he could remember she didn't have that radiant smile on her face. Melissa had become like a second daughter to him. He remembered the look of achievement on her face when she had recovered the polly ball on her first try. All while he bantered on in the background. How she stood up to Michael when he was being an ass. She had really come into her own here in Boothbay Harbor. Everyone by now knew who she was, and she still had fans asking her for selfies and autographs, but for the most part, she was able to make a new life here so far.

"Hey, Hollywood and Jarvis. What are you guys up to?"

"Taking a walk; it's been a crazy day, and it's not even over yet."

"How did Jack handle the news about having a dog?" asked Russell.

"He took it well. He stopped in to check in on us and was all about the dog. What really stopped him was me asking him to move in with me." Melissa responded.

"What do you mean, move in with you?"

"Russell, we are engaged, and I am pregnant with his baby. Don't you think we should live together?"

"Of course, but why not move in with him? Anne is right there to help with the baby if you need it. We like to keep family close. You know that."

"My house is not that far away, Russell."

"What did Jack say when you brought this idea up?"

"He didn't say no, he said he had to think about it?"

"And you, you are dead set on separating our family?"

Melissa had never heard Russell talk to her with such a sharp tone. She paused a bit before answering.

"Russell... I love your family; you of all people should know that, but Jack and I need to have some space. To be on our own."

"Here I am, my time on this planet gettin' shorter, and you want to take my boy from me. Have we ever intruded on your privacy?" He coughed a bit, and Melissa could tell he was struggling for air; she wanted him to calm down, but he kept going. "I thought you were better than that. I thought you loved this family."

Melissa was in tears now. She couldn't believe Russell's tone, his words, his anger. She opened her mouth to say something in hopes of deescalating the situation, but Russell started coughing even more. Coughing hard, so hard blood sprayed, aspirated like a child's squirt gun running out of water. He looked at Melissa, and his eyes rolled back into his head, and he fell towards her. She let go of Jarvis's leash and caught Russell. She screamed at the top of her lungs for help. She could hear him gurgling, so she rolled him to his side. Clive Farrin had heard Melissa's scream and came running. He didn't even ask what was wrong. He immediately called 911.

Chapter 5

Demetri Balfour sat at his oak desk in the corner of a vast warehouse. Not ten feet from his desk, spread out on the floor, was a sheet of 6 mil clear plastic sheeting still attached to a roll suspended on a rolling cart. A chair set, in the middle of the plastic sheet, was stained with blood and had spots worn into it from zip ties that had been under strain. The chair was the peak of the system that he used to control his captures.

New girls and sometimes boys were brought by a box truck. The truck would back into the warehouse, so nobody could see the unloading, and none of the victims had any idea where they were. One of Balfour's men would go into the truck and cut the zip tie that held them in place, then lift them up by their arms, one at a time, and walk them out of the truck. There, in the middle of the warehouse, they would be searched vigorously, stripped to their underwear; all cell phones, watches, purses, identification, and other personal belongings were taken and thrown into a furnace. From there, they were taken to individual holding cells, the size of a closet; no windows, light, or bed. Just a 5-gallon bucket. Balfour had several of these soundproof rooms to hold them. Balfour would select a couple girls that had been there a few days that showed good discipline and have them go talk to and clean up the newcomers. They would calm the girls down and help them put on make-up, and try on dresses, almost a bonding session.

Then, one by one, the newcomers were brought to the chair. Most of the people that sat in the chair would comply just because of the ominous scene. Demitri's men would set them down and zip tie their arms and legs to the chair. Demitri would come into view, much like an evil apparition. He said the same thing to all his guests.

"There is no hope of escape; there is no hope of being found. You will never see your family again. You belong to me now, and I intend to sell you. Items that are broken do not sell well. Do not make me break you. If you do what I ask, you will not be hurt. If you resist, I will hurt you. If you resist too much, I will kill you and roll out some fresh plastic. Now, when my associate cuts you loose, go to the couch and undress slowly for the camera."

It worked every time. With a few words, he removed all hope and replaced it with despair. The chair, the plastic, his thugs, and him. It could be considered brainwashing. First, their clothes are taken off, then they are thrown into a dark room. Then, given some kindness from a peer. Then, bound to a chair and given a menacing ultimatum. The roller coaster of emotions helped instill insecurity and despair.

There had been a few that resisted; they were put in line with gut punches and strikes to the kidneys. One young lady got a full swing and punched one of the thugs once. He choked her to death right there on the spot. Easing his grip so she would die as slowly as possible. Some of the other girls were watching so they could tell any new girls what happened.

After photographing the girls, Balfour would make an ad on his website for his online used furniture store, which was the cover for his human trafficking operation. If the girl was fit, white, blonde-haired, blue eyed, and between the age of 17 and 23, the ad would read, "Like new, light-colored wood, with blue trim chair, price $100." If the girl had dark colored hair and was heavy set and between the age of 23 and 30, the ad would read, "Dark colored recliner, slightly used, $50." The price was multiplied by 1,000. The website even had a "In Search Of" section for those seeking a certain type. When someone wanted to make a purchase, they would call the number on the site. From there, a broker would sort out actual buyers from people stumbling on to the site by asking a series of code questions, which would be answered by code answers. The answers and the questions had nothing to do with each other. The question may be "Where do you live?" and the code question may be "I had tuna for lunch." After both parties were happy with the security, a drop point was agreed upon to transfer pictures of the girl. Once the price had been paid, Balfour would charter a private plane, and the girl would be delivered to the buyer, never to be seen again. As many steps as were involved, it only took a week, at most, from the point of capture to the close of sale.

He rubbed his chin, thinking of how to word his next two ads. For the retired actress Melissa Andrews and the DEA agent Carla Rand, he had to say something different. He would have to put up the ads before they were caught. Maybe even as an auction to maximize the profit. He had no doubt that the actress would bring in at least a million dollars, maybe more. To say she was attractive was an understatement. She was high profile and highly desired. The DEA agent had her own type of value; she was attractive too, but, also represented law and government. Some of his customers would relish a chance to sexually subjugate a representative of the US government. Both would require... training before they became obedient servants, but his clients would enjoy that process. He started a new page on his website named "Special Auction," with the brief description stating, "beautiful and rare furniture requiring refinishing." He smiled at the insinuation. He knew the destiny that awaited Melissa and Carla, and he reveled in it. It would be hard not to... test the furniture, not that he ever did. It was unprofessional and unsafe. These girls were picked up off the street. Some were runaways, others snatched on their way to or from school, some drugged while at a bar or club. One customer wanted a boy and girl about the same age, so his lead thug, Paul, watched a local teen hang out. Not long after watching the little hide away, a young couple matching the customer's requirements parked. Paul dressed himself like a cop and hand cuffed the teens, and put them in the van. He had another thug get the car and bring it to the warehouse.

They would wait a while, then let the car turn up across the country somewhere, making it appear as if the couple had run away. Owning a private shipping company made the logistics of this so easy. He could ship drugs, guns, money, and human beings anywhere on the globe. He was the Amazon of the crime world, hidden in plain sight, right in Portland, Maine. The biggest crime enterprise was tucked away in one of the smallest big cities in the world.

Melissa stared around the waiting room. Everyone's eyes were either staring down at the ground or off into space. She didn't dare to make eye contact with anyone. This was her fault. Why had she even tried to pull Jack away from his family? That was one of the things she loved about him, them, how tight they were. All she wanted was a little separation. She wanted room to learn how to be a wife and mother, room to make mistakes. She didn't want to have Anne, Russell or Lucy running over every time the baby cried. She wanted to make love to Jack without worrying about people listening. She and Jack tended to be a little clamorous. She loathed herself for thinking such things at a time like this. Everything had happened so fast. Her scream and the wave of helplessness. Clive, running over, calling 911. How calm Clive was when he told her to call Anne and Jack. The silence all the way to Portland following the ambulance. What a day it had been to this point. First Zeke Townsand, then bringing Jarvis home, now this. Nobody knew that she was the cause of this. Nobody knew that she was telling Russell about Jack moving in with her. Her bottom lip began to tremble as she fought back the urge to break down and cry. The fight was won when a female doctor walked into the waiting room and said, "Finn Family?"

"Yes, that's us," Anne spoke up.

"Can you follow me into the hallway, please?"

The doctor turned and walked through the double doors she had just come from holding one door for the family to file through. She allowed the door to close after the last family member made it through. She paused and looked around the group until she found Anne's face. "Mrs. Finn?"

"Yes."

"Your husband is alive and breathing. He is heavily sedated and has a breathing tube. We are running a series of tests and when he is more stable, we will be taking him for an MRI. We don't know what is wrong yet; we have been focusing on getting him breathing and stable." Doctor Patrica Cole hated the fact she basically gave information that was not informative. She paused and waited for questions she may not have the answers to.

Anne cleared her throat. "May we go see him?"

"Yes, he is unconscious at the moment, he has a breathing tube and many other tubes and wires you need to be careful of. Otherwise, go give him your love, support, and prayers. I do ask you to go in one at a time, please."

As the family went in one-by-one, Melissa's anxiety got higher and higher. What would she say? What could she say? She could see Anne looking over at her a couple of times. Jack walked out of the room and nodded at Melissa that it was her turn. She took a step toward the door sheepishly. The room had that antiseptic smell of artificial fragrance blended with assorted cleaners and soaps. Her steps seemed to be in cadence with the heart monitor. He was lying there with tubes coming out of him in various places. He looked so pale and lifeless, nothing like he usually looked. Russell always seemed to glow with a fire of life, but now that glow was gone. Her bottom lip quivered increasingly as she tried to think of a coherent sentence, but the moment was too much for her. She began to gush with emotion.

"I am so sorry, Russell. I didn't mean to make you so upset. I was so selfish. It's not that I wanted Jack to myself. I wanted to prove to you and Anne that I could be a good wife and mother without needing any help." She paused a bit to collect herself. Tears were streaming down her cheeks. She rested her head on his chest. "I love you, Russell, and never meant to hurt you. Jack and I can live in Jack's house. Just come back to us." She stayed there for a moment, hoping that her promise would miraculously wake him up. She collected herself before walking back out of the room. Noticing she had left the door open a crack and Anne was standing there. She bent her head down to keep from meeting eyes with anyone. She sat down next to Jack with her arms crossing her own body as if she was holding herself together. Anne saw this and read the body language, but decided to ignore it for now. She stood to address the family.

"While your father is unconscious, I would like a member of the family to stay here. I will take the first shift until tomorrow morning. Lucy and Sam, I will need you to open The Harbor and get it going. Jack, you will probably have to manage the dock. Melissa, can you come up in the morning?"

Melissa nodded her head; she was taken back by Anne's leadership while her husband was in a hospital bed fighting for his life. They all got up to say goodbye to Anne and give her a hug before leaving. Melissa was the last one. She was still staring down at the ground and couldn't look Anne in her eyes.

"Jack, go on down to your truck; Melissa will be right down." Melissa stood frozen and scared. Watching Jack walk away didn't make it easier. "What did you do to my husband?" said Anne in a sharp tone. Melissa was stuttering and trying to find the words. "What did you say to him?" Melissa broke down and felt ashamed; not only did she hurt Russell, but now she was crying in front of Anne who was being so strong.

"I am sorry, Anne; I was just so happy about being pregnant and Jack and I getting married, I didn't think things through. I wanted to show you all that I could be a good mother and wife on my own. I didn't think he would take it so hard." As she took a breath to say more, Anne interrupted.

"Prove to us, or yourself? Melissa, I already know you can do it. So don't let that stubborn old ox in that hospital bed make you feel guilty. He is the only one to blame for being where he is. I have been hounding him to go see a doctor. Just like years ago when I tried to have him give up that god damned pipe. Now, when he wakes up, I am going to pull his head out of his ass. I suggest you do the same. My boy is going to need you, and… I will too." Melissa nodded in agreement, then walked off to catch up with Jack. Anne turned to the door to Russell's room and said, "Look at the mess you made," then sat down and cried her heart out.

Russell lay there with his mind in gear, but his body was stuck in neutral. He heard every word that every family member said, and it tore him apart. He was a loved man and couldn't return it. Now he could hear his wife crying out in the hallway. She had followed the family creed. Be like a duck, calm and peaceful above the surface, paddling like crazy under. She had remained strong for him and the family, and now she was letting loose. The worst part was that she was right. He was at fault for being in this situation. When the "just a cough" lasted 3 weeks, he should have called the doctor. That was months ago. He thought about the warning labels on the pouches of tobacco he stuffed in his pipe with. How stupid do you have to be to inhale something that says it will kill you. Not only that, but society as a whole has condemned it to a degree. If he made it out of this, he was going to throw the pipe and every pack of tobacco he had into the fireplace. If… fuck "if". He was going to fight for every ounce of his being to live through this. He had a grandchild on the way. He had knots to teach, stories to tell, and wisdom to pass. He wanted to watch his son get married. Now lying lifeless in this bed, the thought of Jack moving out of the family compound didn't seem so bad. Christ he would still see him every day practically. Why did he let it get him so riled up, and now poor Melissa was blaming herself. He put his mind to rest and focused on getting better.

Balfour's top man, Paul Kreugar, sat in the Mercedes Benz sedan in the parking lot of The Harbor. The place looked dead. Nobody was around. His assignment was to locate the Hollywood actress, and follow her around, and get an idea on her daily routine. All the social media outlets had been talking about how she was retiring from acting and working for the Finn family at this restaurant. She was also working at the school, but he really couldn't go poking around up there. If she wasn't here, where could she be? He started thumbing through the social media outlets, and sure enough, there she was, coming out of Maine Medical Center in Portland. Someone at the hospital had seen her going in and put a picture of her on Facebook. Now the media was converging like bloodhounds. "God bless social media," Paul said out loud. He kept watching as a video popped up of her boyfriend sheltering her from the press and saying that they were there because of his father and to give his family privacy. Then asking the camera man if he wanted ketchup on his camera before he eats it. The video stopped at that point. But not before showing her boyfriend's truck with the plate number. All he had to do was text his Portland PD friend with the plate number, and he would be able to find out where this man lived. "Progress," he said out loud. He would wait until he was close enough to take a picture of her himself before he would call Mr. Balfour. Then it was just a matter of staying with her. Mr. Balfour didn't want to pick up either Melissa or Carla until he had worked out his plan. But he did want to know their routines and what they were doing. That was actually going to be easy. The press and social media would help keep an eye on Melissa, and the FBI would make it very easy to know where Agent Rand was and what she was doing. A contact in the FBI had told them that an Agent Roberts was watching her and was the lead agent on Dan Ross's case. They even suspected Agent Rand was working with Ross. Paul couldn't have planned that better himself. Their FBI contact was low level, but Balfour already had a plan to get this Agent Roberts on his side. Another concern with Rand was she was an agent herself. She was trained in hand-to-hand combat and probably armed 90 percent of the time. When it came time to grab her, he would have to be careful. A sound from his cell phone broke his thought train. It was the name and address of Ms. Andrew's boyfriend. "Jack Finn... Let's go look at your house."

⁂

Melissa sat quietly in the truck, thinking about what Anne had said. She looked over at Jack, completely emotionless, zoned out, staring out the windshield with one hand on the steering wheel and the other resting on the center console. She slid her hand into his and gave it a squeeze, and when he turned, she gave a warm smile. He was thinking, processing, going over the "what to do's." This was not a time for her to speak, but to let him know she was there, by his side, and ready to help. He took a long, deep breath and let it out slowly. As if to mechanically drain all the bad out. He took another breath and spoke.

"While we are out of town, we ought to get a few things for Jarvis. Dog bed, food bin, toys, treats, and stuff."

Melissa was tempted to remind him that Nick Upham had already brought stuff over from Zeke's house, but she knew what he was doing. He wanted a distraction. "That sounds like a good idea. How about we get some dinner too."

Jack hadn't been hungry until she mentioned it. Now he was starving. He gave her a grin and said, "food first". He thought it odd he could have such levity given the circumstances. But that is what Melissa did for him. A shining light in a dark tunnel. So far, he was holding up pretty good. His father was alive. They didn't know how serious it was yet. If it was cancer, he knew it wouldn't be pretty. It would be a nasty fight. Fight is just what his dad would do, though. He started second guessing the idea of moving out. His mother may need all the help she could get. This wasn't the time to bring that up, though. "Yeah, I usually don't like chain restaurants, but there is an El Rodeo right by the Walmart."

"Tacos sound good about now, Jack."

After their fill of tacos and other Mexican food, they wandered the isles of Walmart. Jarvis was about to be the most spoiled dog in Maine. Their cart was full of random dog toys, a new dog bed, and various other dog items. Somehow, they made their way into the baby section. Melissa fawned over the baby clothes while Jack inspected strollers and car seats. He and Melissa grinned at each other, both caught up in the glee of becoming parents. Until they both came to the breast pumps. They gave each other an awkward look, then burst into laughter.

"Melissa and Jack! What are you doing in the baby section?!" a voice called out.

Jack looked over the display of diapers to see Alyssa Allen looking over at them.

"Jack, is it a reporter?" Melissa asked.

"Oh, it's just Alyssa Allen, you know, selectwoman Alyssa Allen, Chamber of Commerce Alyssa Allen."

"What are we going to do?"

"Just follow my lead," said Jack as he turned to Alyssa. "Hi, Alyssa, how are you doing?"

"I am fine, Jack, now, do you want to tell me what you two are doing here?" Alyssa asked with an inquisitive grin.

"Well, it's a secret... you can't tell anybody," said Jack while Melissa looked on, completely mortified. "My sister is pregnant, and we are shopping for her."

"Oh, that is so nice of you." She turned to Melissa. "How are you doing, settling into Boothbay Harbor?"

"It's going great. I love the town and its people."

"You are one of its people now. Well, I have to finish up my shopping here. See you guys later."

"Bye, Alyssa," said Jack.

"Your sister is going to kill us."

"Alyssa is good people, she won't tell anyone."

"You better hope not. I will be throwing you right under that bus."

Chapter 6

Pulling into Melissa's driveway, they saw a new car they hadn't seen before. They had asked for Lizzy to come check on Jarvis, but this wasn't her car, nor was it Michael's or Abigail's. Jack was slightly concerned. Even though Melissa had stopped acting, she was still a celebrity, and sometimes fans or reporters didn't respect personal boundaries. He told Melissa to stay in the truck while he checked things out. He walked up to the door slowly and steadily. The door to Melissa's house opened, and Jarvis came running out to greet him. Jack breathed a sigh of relief as Abigail stepped out onto the porch. "I guess he knows who his new family is," closing the door behind her.

"That's what Finns do, take in the strays!" said Melissa, proud of the joke, even if it was at her expense.

"Lizzy had schoolwork this evening, so I told her I would come watch Jarvis. It was a great treat. He is such a good dog."

They updated Abigail on Russell's condition, and Abigail let them know that the Williams family would be there for whatever support they needed, especially if it meant watching Jarvis. Abigail explained that with Lizzy now driving and Josh either riding with her or one of his friends, she no longer needed a minivan and had bought herself a new car. After exchanging hugs and goodbyes, Jack and Melissa went inside the house.

The sun was just starting to set; Jack and Melissa decided they could get a walk in with their new family member before it got too dark. Jarvis was outfitted with his new gear. A collar with a GPS locator and a new leash. Jack, still wanting to keep the mood positive, decided to bring up a topic that would keep them both happy.

"So, let's think about baby names!" Jack said.

"Too late. I already have them picked out."

"What do you mean, them?"

"One girl name and one boy name."

"Don't I have a say in this?"

"Of course you do, but something tells me you will love the names I have picked out."

"Ok… what ya got?"

"Jacqueline Anne Finn." She paused a bit, knowing the boy's name was going to hit home. "Russell Michael Finn".

Jack stopped in his tracks and tried to swallow the lump forming in his throat. She was right. He loved the names. He couldn't speak, and she could see it. She slowly wrapped her arms around him and rested her head on his chest. After looking over the water at Barrett's park they continued on their walk. Melissa loved moments like this, despite the early spring chill in the air, holding on to Jack made her warm. The red sky in the evening looked like the horizon was on fire. The only sounds were the cold breeze and the sounds of calling seagulls. They continued their walk along Lobster Cove Road as Jack gave Melissa more history of the area. Pointing to houses and saying who used to live there. The Begin's, Trask's, the Sellick's and many others. All with a short story. "Their daughter used to babysit me," "He had a dog named Blueberry," or "I went to school with their daughter; her name was Melissa too." In Boothbay Harbor, everyone mattered in one way, shape, or form, and though you might not know everyone, you knew someone that knew someone that knew that person. Melissa had noticed long ago that everyone was recognized by either their family or their occupation. She remembered a conversation between Clive and Russell as they would try to figure out who they were talking about.

"Isn't that Johnny's grandson?"

"Nope, Johnny's grandson works at Hannaford's. The guy you're talking about is a carpenter for Steve Malcom and is married to Bernice's daughter."

Melissa was in awe of how these people could keep track of one another. They had made the turn to go up what Jack called "hawse hill" or, as it was really pronounced, "horse hill". It was a steep hill that made her calves burn by the time they got to the top. They talked about anything they could to avoid talking about Russell and his situation, though it was still on both of their minds. Jarvis was a great walking dog. Just trotting along beside them, occasionally stopping to point at a squirrel or chipmunk.

"Jack, do you want to know what the baby is? Or do you want it to be a surprise."

"Well part of me wants it to be a surprise. Then the other part wants to know, so I know what color to paint the baby's room, and what clothes to get, and what color stroller.

"You are really getting into this aren't you?"

"I have been googling all kinds of stuff. You know they have little themed strollers. Disney princess ones and John Deere tractor ones."

Melissa laughed a bit. It felt good that Jack was into having a baby and looking into things. "I think the room that is my office will make a good nursery. It's close to the bedroom. Have you thought about the wedding at all? You know that is coming first."

"Yup, Michael is going to be my best man and will have his boat available. He and I will build a platform to put on my boat so we will be up where everyone can see us. Have you asked Lizzy about being your maid of honor?"

"No not yet. That girl is busy and hard to get a hold of. I think I will take her out to lunch and ask her. I see Josh a bit. He auditioned to be in the school play."

"Are you serious, Josh? What part did he audition for?"

"The lead, he is going to be Marty McFly in the Back to the Future musical."

"Wow, Michael didn't even mention it."

"That is because Michael doesn't know."

"What do you mean he doesn't know?"

"Josh wants to keep it a secret; you know how Michael is. He doesn't think much of the entertainment industry. I think Josh is worried about what Michael will think about him singing and acting."

"Michael is coming around...slowly. He may feel a little hurt that everyone kept this secret from him. Josh is his son. I know he would love that kid if he was rebuilding engines, flipping burgers, or singing on stage."

"Ok, you have a good point. I will talk to Josh about it."

"How is he? I mean, is he any good?"

"Good? He is awesome. I have been working with him on his voice, but he has acting down."

"The kid would sing a bit on the boat. It sounded pretty good."

"Yeah, singing along with the radio and singing without is totally different. I am teaching him some pitch control and how to push his voice outward. You should see him on stage, though. The pauses, the gestures, he can even improvise on the fly when something doesn't go right."

There was a bit of silence while they thought about telling Michael. Melissa decided to break the silence and change the subject.

"Back to the wedding, Michael is going to be your best man, Josh a groomsman. I will have Lizzy as my maid of honor and Abigail as a bridesmaid."

"Are you going to have dad give you away?"

"Yes," said Melissa with worry in her voice.

"Dad will pull through. I just know he will. He is too stubborn to stop now. Especially with a grandkid coming. Not to mention the chance to walk you down the aisle."

With that they walked holding each other. Giving each other comfort and assurance. Both of them, starting to get a little overwhelmed. Zeke passing, Jarvis, pregnancy, marriage, and now Russell in the hospital. They returned to the house and turned in for the night, putting an end to a terrible day.

Jack woke up to his alarm and gave Melissa a peck on the cheek. He noticed that, during the night, Jarvis had gotten up from his dog bed in the living room and had climbed up onto Melissa's side of the bed and curled up in a little ball by her legs. He gave Jarvis a pat on the head and then whispered, "That is not always going to work, bud." Jack getting ready in the morning was something like watching a NASCAR pit crew. He prided himself on how fast he could get out of the house. Clothes all set aside; the coffee maker set to start brewing so it would be done by the time he was ready to go. This morning was a little different, Melissa had set out a Hannaford shopping bag with Jarvis's food, a toy, and a few treats. "She is already acting like a mother," Jack said to himself. He tried to whisper for Jarvis to come. No sound of paws on the hardwood floor. Up the stairs he went. "Jarvis" he called in a loud whisper. Jarvis looked up at Jack with a facial expression as if to say "What?" Jack chuckled a bit "Come on, Jarvis, you're with me today. She will be fine." The dog looked over at Melissa, sound asleep, then back at Jack. There was a moment of pause, as if Jarvis was going to rebel and go back to sleep. Instead, he got up, grumbling a bit. Jack had to bite his lip to not laugh at the dog's disposition. Jarvis led Jack out the door, then to his truck, staring at the door as if to say, "Come on, you got me out of bed; now let's get going." Jarvis hopped up into the truck and sat on the passenger side. The two were off for their first day of work together.

Carla Rand woke up in her hotel bed wearing the same clothes she had worn yesterday. She needed to take a shower and change. At the same time, she knew her apartment was being watched by the FBI and Balfour's men. "What a fucking mess you left, Dan," she said out loud. As she said it, the emotions started to flush. At first, she was going to put up her wall and hold them back. Not now; she had to let this go. She curled up in a ball and cried. She had fallen in love with Dan, and he was lying to her the whole time. Did he ever have feelings for her, or was he just using her? What was his plan? Was he going to kill her? Even from the grave, he was hurting her. Hurting her career. Her big bust, the biggest bust Maine had ever seen, was now tainted. An asterisk would be in her record even if cleared of this. She rolled on to her back, staring up at the ceiling. At least she, Roberts, and Stryker had the beginning of a plan. She just had to stay hidden until they were ready. She would be doing a lot of counter surveillance from here on out. She had to be sharp and ready. She sat up on that notion and started to gather herself, partially ashamed of her crying fit. Then came a knock at the door. First three knocks, then two, then one. The code she, Roberts, and Stryker had set. If it had been in the opposite order, it meant they were under duress. She checked the peep hole anyway and saw Agent Roberts' bright red hair. She opened the door to let him in. He came in holding shopping bags from Walmart and Old Navy. He put them down on the hotel bed and looked at Agent Rand with a red face.

"Look…this is awkward. I don't know you that well, and these are pretty fucked up circumstances, as it is." He motioned to the bags on the bed. She opened the Wal-Mart bag to find women's underwear and bras in her sizes.

"How did you know my size?" she asked aggressively.

"This is one of those things you start doing that seems like a nice gesture at first, then goes kind of south. I knew you didn't have any extra clothes or anything. I knew your sizes from searching your apartment. So, I figured I would go to the store and get you some… stuff. The shampoo, conditioner, toothpaste and brush were easy. Picking you out a couple outfits was kind of weird. Buying you underwear and bras is where I started having second thoughts, but I figured you needed them. With your house under surveillance, I didn't want to be seen getting you a change of clothes. I will go wait in my car. You need to go to your office and see what the DEA is going to do with you."

The embarrassment of having a man she had just met buy her underwear was replaced with the anxiety of losing her job. She wasn't sure if Andy Roberts was the big or little brother she never had, but in some strange way, she was glad she was going through this with him.

"Andy, thank you. I will be right out."

"Take your time… you need a good shower," Agent Roberts said as he made a gesture to his nose and walked out with a devious grin on his face. The shower and fresh clothes felt good. The outfits that Andy had picked out made her look more like a teenager on her first day of high school rather than an agent of the law. She walked out of the hotel and scanned the parking lot. She could see Agent Roberts in his BMW. She walked to the car she had borrowed from the DEA motor pool. The ride to her office was uneventful. She could see agent Roberts was following her. At a stoplight, he sent a text that he was going to check in, that he had found her, and was tailing her.

When she got to her office, she found that the keypad combination had already been changed. There was a note on the door for her to report to her supervisor. Her supervisor's door was open, she knocked on the door casing to get his attention. He looked up and saw her, and his face went stern.

"Come in, sit down," he said, as if talking to a dog.

"You wanted to see me, sir?"

"Yes, put your service weapon and badge on my desk. You are now on paid administrative leave. During the course of the investigation, you are to stay in the state of Maine. If cleared, you will be put under review, if you pass review, you can have your badge and gun back. The FBI will be monitoring your every move until you are cleared."

"Sir…."

"There is no discussion; this is happening. Clear your weapon, put it on my desk, along with your badge. Then get out of my office."

Another agent stepped in and rested his hand on his sidearm while Agent Rand removed her weapon. She removed the magazine, cycled the slide, catching the round. She didn't even bother to put the round back in the magazine. She put the gun, round, and magazine on his desk. She removed the badge from her belt and put it on top of everything. She wanted to yell that she was innocent right into his face, but that wouldn't do any good. She turned and walked out, almost running into the agent that was watching. Leaving the building was like walking through a gauntlet. Everybody staring, speculating, thinking she was a dirty agent that got another agent killed. She got into her car and found a cell phone sitting in the cup holder. She looked at it while closing her door, almost scared to touch it, then it beeped. She picked it up and looked at the screen. The contact was two letters, *AR*, the text read.

Your phone is being monitored. They had me put a GPS locator on your car. What is your plan?

She texted back: *FBI is watching my apartment, right?*

Yes, two agents, all the time, plus a rover, and me.

Then I guess it will be safe then. I will hang there for a while.

Good plan.

Carla thought for a moment. Then texted back: *Thank you, Andy.*

She then texted Commissioner Stryker and let him know her new number and what was going on. Before going to her apartment, she went to Best Buy and picked up some GPS tags, and a case for the phone agent Roberts got her. She placed a tag on her car, another in her purse, another inside the case for her phone before putting her phone in. She made a stop at a drugstore and bought a pack of Band-Aids. She stuck the last tag on the gauze side of a Band-Aid, then stuck it up under her arm, up by her armpit. She turned on the app, then named all tags. Car, purse, phone, and body. She shared the link with Roberts and Stryker. She wasn't sure if Balfour had anyone else from the FBI on his payroll or would be recruiting people. This way, Roberts and Stryker would always know where she was. The next part of what she had to do was the hardest. Sit and wait; she would have to go home and just wait for something to happen.

Lizzy came down the steps from her bedroom, ready to raid the cereal cabinet. She found her father sitting at the dinner table with a cup of coffee and a bagel.

"Good morning, Daddy, why are you still here?"

"I wanted to talk to you about something. Get your breakfast, then come join your old man for a bit."

Lizzy sat down with a bowl of cereal and a cup of hot cocoa. Michael smiled at the sight. She had sat in that very chair, sometimes in a booster seat, and ate her breakfast with him on many occasions while growing up.

"Lizzy, I talked to Melissa a little after we got done shooting the other day. She never got to go to a high school prom. I got an idea. You need to get her to volunteer to be a chaperone for the prom. I will take care of the rest."

"What are you thinking, Daddy?"

"I don't know yet, but the wheels are spinning, and a plan is starting."

"That will be easy; she likes being involved at the school, and we are going to ask Agent Rand to chaperone, too, due to the missing kids lately. That will take care of our female chaperones. The students and teachers like her. I am on the prom committee, so I can help a bit too."

"What do you mean, we?"

"I am on the Prom committee."

"Prom committee! Lizzy, when are you going to slow down a bit? You work at The Harbor, then school, then swim practice, then homework, somewhere in there you get dinner."

"Just following you and mommy's example. You guys used to work so hard, we barely saw both of you at the same time. I remember you working out in the shop and me or Josh bringing dinner out to you."

"Lizzy, I did that because I had to. Nothing wrong with having a strong work ethic, but don't forget to have some fun now and then.

"Funny you should bring that up. I would like to go out to the movies Friday?"

"You know I have no problem with that. Who are you going with? Hazel Westin?

"Um… no, I was asked to go to the movies by a boy."

Michael swallowed his sip of coffee a little harder. He took in the moment, knowing it was going to happen sooner or later. He was actually kind of surprised it hadn't happened before now. He was dating when he was a freshman, this was Lizzy's senior year. He relaxed his body slowly and looked over at his daughter. She was watching him, she was playing a game of chess with him, anticipating his words and getting ready for his next move. He decided to make a surprise move.

"What is the boy's name?"

Lizzy hadn't expected that. She was expecting a debate or the "got to talk to your mother about this." response. She had almost forgotten the young man's name.

"His name is Liam, Liam Deene. You know his dad."

"Oh yeah, Jeff's boy. I sold him a Scania a couple years ago. He is a senior too, right."

"Yes, he is on the honor roll as well and on the math club. He…"

"Lizzy, Lizzy, Lizzy." Michael interrupted. "You don't have to sell him to me, but he does have to sell himself. If he is going to take my daughter to the movies, he needs to come and have dinner with us. Sometime this week. You let your mother know as well, ok."

Lizzy beamed with happiness. She didn't think it was going to go this easy. "Yes, Daddy." She finished her cereal and gave her father a hug and a kiss on the cheek. "Love you, Daddy."

"Love you too kiddo." He waited until she left, and let out a big sigh.

Anne hadn't opened her eyes yet. She was awake and could hear Russell's ventilator and heart monitor. She kept her eyes shut in some effort to make this all a dream. Maybe if she kept her eyes shut a little longer, she would wake up in her bed, in her house, next to Russell. The other reason she sat there in this awake but asleep state was she knew by sleeping in that chair all night, the minute she tried to move, all her muscles and joints would retaliate from sleeping in a chair. She heard the door to the room open and figured it was the nurse making her rounds. Then she smelled something... something good. She cracked open one eye to see Melissa had set a box, a take-out food box, on the table and was taking stuff out of a bag and setting it on the table as well. Anne looked up on the table and found Melissa had brought Anne some things from home. Not just stuff for Anne but pictures and small plants. Melissa had obviously seen the grin on Anne's face, because she herself was grinning too. Yet Melissa didn't try to engage with her. She let her sit there and come to on her own time.

"I smell you found Becky's Diner," said Anne with her eyes still closed.

"Yes, I got you a bacon, onion, and cheese omelet with a side of bacon and an English muffin. I made the coffee myself this morning, knowing how strong you like it."

Anne opened both of her eyes and slowly sat up. "You had me at bacon. What time is it?"

"Eight o'clock. I left Boothbay Harbor shortly after Jack left the house. Any change?" she said, gesturing towards Russell.

"No, the ox is still sleeping away. Ain't I going to give him some shit when he wakes up."

Obviously, Anne had her strong face on today, Melissa thought to herself. Should she try to open that door, or, let Anne open it? Her question was answered by Anne.

"Melissa, I cried my eyeballs out last night. Cried like a little girl who just lost her stuffy. Russell and I have built one hell of a life together. We have been through hell and back. We raised two kids to adulthood, anxiously awaiting to be grandparents. We were planning on taking the car out next month and going for a cruise. He only had a chance to drive it in the driveway." Anne started to break down a bit.

"Anne, we don't know anything yet. This could be as simple as pneumonia or a minor lung infection. If it is worse, we will handle it together. Russell may be old, but that man is tough. Maine lobsterman tough. They don't go down without a fight." She put a hand on Anne's shoulder and gave a gentle squeeze. Anne put her fork down and reached for one of Melissa's hands. She grabbed it gently and gave it a squeeze back. She then cleared her throat and changed the subject.

"When is Jack moving in with you?"

"We haven't discussed that yet. He seems to be more focused on the baby. He has been looking at strollers and stuff. Kind of fun watching him glow at the thought of being a dad. We are going to turn my office area into a nursery and started planning on building on to the house. I know we are getting ahead of ourselves; this could all be for naught. I have an appointment in a couple weeks. Then it will be official, but I have stopped drinking wine and beer, just to be safe."

"Do you have any questions? I mean, I have been through it before… twice."

"Oddly enough, I don't have any. I mean, not yet. I don't want to ask the obvious questions like, does it hurt? I have seen enough videos to know it's not a walk in the park. I know morning sickness will be happening in a month or so. It feels strange to say this, but I feel like I am ready for being pregnant."

"That is not strange at all. You are a strong, confident woman. Just don't let that confidence get in your way. Ask for help when you need it. When you have an eight-to-twelve-pound basketball hanging off your belly and you have to pick up something from the floor, don't be afraid to ask for help. Once that baby is born, you will be fighting with me, Lucy, and that ox over there for time to hold it. Then sometimes you will be glad to have some time to yourself."

Russell lay in bed listening to the conversation. If he could smile, he would. He still had this god-damned breathing tube shoved down his grocery hole. He had heard the nurse would check to see if he could breathe on his own and if so, the tube would be removed. Then off to the MRI to see what was going on. He kept trying to move a finger or toe or something but couldn't. He could hear, though, and that was a reward and a punishment. He could hear this great conversation between Melissa and Anne. They were no longer bonding; they were bonded. In a strange but beautiful hybrid mother friend relationship that had started less than a year ago. Since June, when Jack found Melissa hanging on to a kayak for dear life, the two had been on a fast track of love and passion. It didn't come without a few bumps. They had had a few arguments, a few issues getting over things in their past, and there would be more. Living together puts a strain on a relationship. Having a baby certainly puts any relationship to the test. A baby, Russell paused his thoughts. He was going to be a grandfather. His body tingled a bit at the thought. He didn't care if it was going to be a girl or a boy. He just wanted a little one to spoil and to play with.

"Anne, look… I think Russell is trying to smile!"

Anne looked at her husband, and sure enough, his mouth was attempting to smile around the breathing tube. "He can probably smell this breakfast."

They laughed a little then Dr. Cole came into the room. "I see he is smiling, that is a good sign. Soon we will try taking off the ventilator, then to the MRI. You will have to leave the room when we remove the ventilator."

"How soon, doctor?" Anne asked.

"In a couple of hours, we will shut off the ventilator and see how well he is breathing on his own. We will give him a couple hours to see if he remains stable. Then we will roll him down to the MRI room and take a look at his lungs. His bloodwork came back good."

"Anne, why don't you go home, I will call you when they shut off the ventilator. That way, you can be here when he goes to the MRI."

"Home sounds good. You have the wheel, Melissa."

Chapter 7

.

Paul pulled into The Harbor. He was sore and tired from staying in his car all night. He had watched the address that was Jack Finn's but never saw Jack or anybody. This morning, he figured he would try The Harbor and see if he could spot anybody. All he had to do was walk around and look lost, like a tourist. If someone saw him, he would ask for Jack. After visually verifying Jack, he would say he was a reporter and would likely be shooed away. Unremembered and quickly dismissed.

A large truck had backed onto the dock and started to unload dead fish. The smell was disgusting. At first, Paul thought he could handle it. He tried to breathe from his mouth, but then it seemed he could taste the rancid fish. His stomach started to lurch. He was biting his tongue, resisting the urge to vomit. His eyes started to water, and he lost focus. A man in his 30's had gotten off a fork truck to come to him, but it was too late. Paul vomited all over the dock and the man's boots.

Jack was picking up from the morning rush of boats. Early spring wasn't as busy as a summertime morning rush, but it was still enough to keep Jack busy. Jarvis followed him around the dock and made a sport of barking at the seagulls and scaring them away. The fellow lobstermen were glad to see Jarvis in good hands and happy to see him down at the dock. Zeke's family would be arriving today, and Clive was working on organizing the boat parade in Zeke's honor. Jack was on the fork truck unloading totes of bait when he noticed a strange man walking around. He appeared to be lost and searching for someone. He decided to go ask the guy if he needed help.

"You alright?" Jack asked the man, who was hunched over vomiting. He felt foolish asking. The guy had just puked all over Jack's boots. Good thing they were his Grunden's boots for lobstering. He could hose those and the dock off pretty easily. What was odd to Jack was that Jarvis was growling at the man. Jarvis never growled at anyone.

"Could I get a paper towel or something?" Paul asked.

Jack noted a Russian accent; he remembered how the Russian woman that Tommy worked for sounded.

"Oh sure,"

Jack grabbed a roll of paper towels from the fork truck and pulled off a couple of sheets. He then passed them to the man, still hunched over with his hands on his knees. Paul took the paper towels and wiped his face while standing up. He looked over at the man helping, and sure enough, it was Jack Finn; he recognized him from the TV and papers. Unfortunately for Paul, any pre-arranged strategy he had planned left with the contents of his stomach. He had forgotten to hide his accent, and now he stood there dumbfounded on what to do next. He still had the taste of vomit in his mouth and the smell of it in his nose. If he hadn't just emptied his stomach, he would be vomiting more. He had what he wanted now; he knew where Jack was and soon, after some surveillance, he would see his actual target. He decided to simply walk away from the situation. He walked away quickly and briskly. Leaving his mess behind, and Jack standing there, confused.

Must have been embarrassed, Jack thought to himself, and grabbed the hose to clean off the dock and his boots. Jack looked up at the parking lot and saw the man getting into a large Mercedes sedan. Though it wasn't strange to see a high-end Mercedes in Boothbay Harbor, this time of year it wasn't common. Jack looked at the license plate and spoke it out loud. "62823". He stood there, pondering the events that just happened and weighed them against what had happened last year. There was something nagging for him to do something. "Should I contact Agent Rand?" He thought to himself. "And tell her what, some Russian dude just puked on his boots and took off." Normally, Jack would have let this go, but not with the events of last summer. He took out his phone and called Agent Rand.

"Hello Jack, how are you?'

"I am good. How are you doing?"

"…. I am doing alright. What can I do for you, Jack?" Carla Rand decided not to go into the details of what had been going on. Not to mention that this phone was being monitored.

"Look, this is probably nothing, but a guy came down to the dock just now and puked on my boots and dock, then jumped back into a Mercedes and left."

"Well, not going to argue that that is odd, but why are you calling me about it?"

"The guy had a Russian accent. He came down here, puked, looked at me, and left. It just didn't sit right with me, so I figured I would call you. I got his plate number if you want it."

"Yeah, what is it?"

"Maine plates, 62823."

"Thanks Jack; it's probably nothing, but with Lizzy's involvement in the case and you and Melissa are often in the headlines, I want to be sure. It is easy for someone to connect the dots."

"OK," said Jack with a little anxiety in his voice. "Should I tell Michael?"

"No, no reason to start a panic. I will run this number and see what comes up. I will call Michael myself if I have any concerns for Lizzy. Hey, speaking of you, Melissa, and the news, I saw you guys on the news last night. How is your dad?"

"Well....he is unconscious at the moment, and we are waiting for test results. Mom stayed with him all night and Melissa shot up there this morning to give her a break. Thanks for asking; did you know the FBI guy that died? The news didn't say his name."

"Jack, I can't comment on that right now, Jack. Give your family my best, and your dad will be in my prayers. I will be down that way shortly. I need some more Harbor time."

"Alrighty then, Agent Rand. Have a good one."

"Bye, Jack"

Carla Rand knew that the FBI was listening in on that conversation and was already running those plates. Fifteen minutes later, her other phone, the one that Andy had given her, received a text message.

Plate number comes back to a Paul Kreugar. He is clean and suspicious. No records, no online profile, no info at all. Just basic info.

"Great...can't get a warrant with that," Carla said to herself. Would Balfour go after Lizzy? What did Dan tell Balfour? What can I do with all this, she continued her internal monologue, was this Russian guy the John Smith that visited Tommy? Did they have Lizzy and Melissa confused? It seemed unlikely, but possible. Both were blonde and attractive. Lizzy certainly looked older than 18 and Melissa could pass for someone in their 20's. One thing about Lizzy is that she was aware of her environment. If someone was following her, she would know. Lizzy was a star agent in the making.

***

Lizzy walked into the prom committee meeting and took a seat. They were having their meetings early in the morning before first period so as not to interrupt the school day or afternoon sports and activities. Mrs. Hersom, the science teacher, started off the meeting.

"As this is the first meeting, I will start this off by just laying down some ground rules. After this, it is yours to run, and I just monitor. You have $500 in the budget, but you can raise money to increase your budget. Due to the number of children and people going missing across Maine and New England, the Principal, Mrs. Niles, insists that we have law enforcement at the prom. We also insist that you have two male chaperones and two female chaperones. The law enforcement officer can count as one of them. It's up to you to make the phone calls and emails and all the other organization."

Lizzy, already thinking that she wanted Melissa to chaperone, was considering Agent Rand as the law enforcement and maybe get Uncle Jack and Sam. "I think I have chaperones figured out. I just have to double check."

"Lizzy, would you mind asking if the chaperones would dress up as well? That way they blend in, and we don't feel like we are being babysat," one of the girls asked.

Lizzy didn't know the details of her father's plan, but this could certainly work in her favor. "Sure, I don't think any of them would mind."

"Lizzie is taking care of chaperones, I will work on a venue, any suggestions?" Hazel Westin, Lizzy's best friend, asked.

Suggestions started flowing and details started coming together. At the end of the meeting, all responsibilities of planning had been gone over and tasks assigned. Lizzy walked out of the classroom to find Liam Deene waiting for her across the hall.

"Did you talk to your dad? Can we go out Friday?"

"Well, we are all good to go out to the movies on Friday, except one thing."

"What is that?"

"Dad says you have to come over for dinner."

Liam's face flushed; "H-h-ho-how a-a-a-am I-I-I going t-t-t-to d-d-d-do th-th-th-that?"

Lizzy knew this was going to happen. Liam had a stutter. It was significantly worse if he was stressed or anxious. She was going to try to say he would be fine and had nothing to worry about. Instead of using empathy, she tried a different approach.

"Well, if you want to take me to the movies, you have to have dinner with my family. I will tell my mother you will be over tomorrow night. Now I can come pick you up or have your mom drop you off. If you don't show up, we will not be going to the movies."

Lizzy turned and walked down the hall towards her locker. Liam stood there, considering what he was going to do. He had never spoken to Michael Williams before. His dad knew him and said good things about him. He had been friends with Lizzy for a while now, and, with her going off to college, it was time to ask her out. He never expected to have to have dinner with her family. He could talk to Lizzy without stuttering. Not that she cared; she was always patient and would wait for him to get the words out. Then, with the more time they spent together, the more he felt comfortable. Now he would have to sit at a table with her parents and her brother. Her father sitting right there, sizing him up, but he really liked Lizzy. He would go to dinner.

Lizzy was out in the hall getting her books for class when Hazel Westin came up.

"Hi Lizzy, who are you thinking of for chaperones?

"Melissa and Jack, Sam, and for law enforcement, I was thinking Agent Rand. All of them are younger and, you know, cool. I think that will work better than having someone's parents watching."

"That would be awesome! So, did you talk to your dad about Liam asking you to the movies?"

"Yes, and he was OK with it, but Liam has to come over for dinner first. I just told Liam, and he started stuttering at the thought of it, and he never stutters with me."

"What are you going to do?"

"I decided to play hardball and told him if he wanted to go to the movies, he had to come over for dinner. He has until Thursday night to make up his mind."

"What do you think he will do?"

"I don't know."

"Well…I know what he will do," said Hazel as she looked at Liam, who was now standing next to Lizzy. "I have riding lessons after school, but I will call you after that, okay?"

"Okay, talk to you later."

Lizzy closed her locker and turned towards Liam, waiting for him to speak.

"I will come to dinner; I will have my parents drop me off." Liam said, only stuttering a little.

"Great, any allergies or things you don't like I need to tell my mother about?"

"Nope, I eat just about anything."

"Great, I will let her know. Bye, see you later."

"Bye." said Liam, remembering how much he hated peas. What were the chances they would have peas?

⁂

Melissa sat in the chair, listening to Russell breathe. The ventilation machine had been turned off, and Russell had been breathing on his own for an hour. Dr. Cole told Melissa that there was a scheduling issue and it would be another couple of hours before they could get an MRI done. Melissa updated Anne via text so as not to wake her; well, she hoped Anne was sleeping.

Melissa snuck down to the maternity wing. She felt foolish walking around with the hood up, baseball hat on, and big sunglasses, but she just couldn't take a chance of being caught. She was curious and wanted to take a look. She walked through the doors and spotted an empty seat just across the room. She walked over, and sat down, and started surveying the room. To her right, there was a woman that had the signature large belly; she was leaning back in her chair, enjoying a moment of sitting down. Beside her, there was a young girl, toddler, playing with some dolls. Melissa smiled at the little girl, and she smiled back. The mother turned and looked at Melissa. This couldn't be anymore awkward, Melissa thought. Here she was in a hoodie, sunglasses, and a baseball hat. What she must look like to this woman. But the lady, who was now looking more closely, smiled at Melissa.

"You may want to cover up that logo on your sweatshirt." The woman whispered into Melissa's ear. "Most people in Maine know the boat *Old Smoke*."

Melissa looked down at her shirt, and sure enough, not only did it have Russell's boat on it, but it also said, "First Mate Melissa." Melissa slowly lifted her arm and rested her hand on her shoulder, covering up the embroidery.

"Thank you." She whispered back.

"No problem; my husband and I are big fans, and I can guess why you would want to be here in secret."

"It's not official yet, and only Jack knows. I was just curious and wanted to come down. I didn't really plan this out very well."

"Your secret is safe with me; I won't even tell my husband until he comes back from Iraq."

A lump formed in Melissa's throat. This woman wasn't only pregnant and had a toddler; her husband was fighting a war. She wanted to do or say something. The young woman recognized the pause and passed the magazine she was reading towards Melissa, then dug in her purse for a pen. The magazine was turned into a picture taken of her and Jack at the boat races. One of the many articles that had been done since the summer. Melissa smiled at her and signed the picture, then wrote her number on the back.

"You and your husband call me as soon as he gets home, okay?"

Melissa was about to get up when the young woman motioned for her to stay for a moment. She reached into her purse again and pulled out a book about pregnancy.

"I have already done it once; you take it. Make sure Jack reads the part for fathers."

"Thank you."

The young woman nudged her daughter, "Maddie, can you tell the nice lady the name of your dolls?"

The little girl held up two dolls; one was a woman, the other a man. "This is Jack and Melissa."

Melissa smiled at both of them and walked out of the room.

When Melissa got back to Russell's room, she started looking at the book the woman had given her. Taking mental notes of all the dos and don'ts,she decided she would work right up to when she went into labor if she could. It would keep her busy and her mind occupied. The thought that a life was starting within her made her warm. She would be bringing another life into this world. Another Finn in the family. A child to raise with the best possible family supporting her and Jack. They would be sharing first words, first steps, first day of school, and more. She knew it was early to have these thoughts, but she couldn't help herself.

The moment was interrupted when she heard a scuffling outside of the door. Not a fight, but certainly some type of confrontation. She decided to take a look. Keeping the pregnancy book in her left hand and tucked behind her, she went to the door and opened it. Once she did, she realized her mistake. A flash of light caught her by surprise, followed by several people asking an overwhelming fountain of questions. Just before stepping out into the hallway, she realized she had a pregnancy book in her left hand. She gave it a toss into the corner, and stepped into the hallway, and closed the door. She took a deep breath and poised herself. Then let go.

"What is wrong with you people? Jack's father is lying in that room fighting for his life, and you people are so selfish that you come up here and disturb the staff that are trying to render care to sick people! You are the reason I left Hollywood. You are so consumed with getting a story that you don't even care about an individual's right to privacy. Are you telling the people that your headlines are more important than the lives of the patients on this floor?"

One short blond reporter with a pixie haircut and dark rimmed glasses pushed her way to the front and said in a semi nasal tone, "Celebrities give up their privacy when they become famous."

Melissa turned to her and said, "Say pop."

"Pop," the reporter said in a confused tone.

"Good, that was the sound of your head coming out of your ass."

The crowd chuckled a bit, but the reporter refused to back off. She had noticed that the sweatshirt Melissa was wearing had a small tear in it and decided that would be good fodder for insult.

"Do you know there is a hole in your shirt?"

"Do you know there is an asshole in yours?" Melissa fired back quickly.

With that, Melissa turned and went back into Russell's room. She heard the hospital security shuffling the reporters out. She sat down, relieved that there were no questions about pregnancy. Dr. Cole came in and first apologized for the disturbance, then told Melissa they would be preparing Russell for the MRI in a couple hours. Melissa texted Anne to let her know.

Anne got in her car as soon as she got the text. She had gotten some sleep but not nearly as much as she needed. The MRI would dictate the rest of their lives. If he had cancer, how long did he have? What would they do with that time? Would they try to fight it with chemo or other treatments that would lower his quality of life? Or would he just live the best life he could until the cancer won? Did cancer really win or lose? If Russell chose to live his life with no treatment, was he giving up? All these questions she asked herself but had no answers. The drive to Portland was normally an hour and a half, but it felt like forever. She didn't turn on the radio. She wanted the silence.

When Anne arrived, Russell had been off the ventilator for three hours and breathing well on his own. Dr. Cole told them that they may remove the breathing tube after the MRI and start bringing him out of the coma. Melissa and Anne were told they would have to wait in the lobby while they did the MRI. Melissa sent a group text to Lucy, Jack, and the Williams to let them know the status. Sam and Lucy volunteered to stay with Russell for the night. It had seemed like an eternity had passed when Dr. Cole came into the waiting room.

"Mrs. Finn, I have an update on your husband's condition." She paused a bit while she let Anne and Melissa take a breath. "With the tests we have conducted and using the MRI as a backstop, we have determined that your husband has a lower respiratory infection, more commonly known as pneumonia. The case is severe but treatable. We will be removing the breathing tube but putting him on oxygen; he will be getting antibiotics and fluids through an IV. My goal is to give him back to you by the end of this week. Then routine follow ups every week for about a month. After that, his PCP can handle it."

"After he gets home… how do we take care of him? I mean, what are the do's and don'ts?

"He must give up smoking his pipe. That is your first battle. Other than that, make sure to wear proper protection around any dust or fumes. That means when sanding and painting his buoys. Even around saw dust." She paused again to let Anne have a moment of thought. "Mrs. Finn, you and your family have had a big scare, but your husband is going to be around for a long time."

Melissa held Anne, and she could feel the tension fade away. Anne put her head on Melissa's shoulder, and she could hear Anne say, "My Russell."

Dr. Cole went on to say that Russell would be coming out of a coma. Due to the breathing tube, it would be a while before he could talk. Anne joked that it was probably better for everyone.

Russell could hear the words being spoken around him. The relief of being cancer free was almost euphoric. He knew he had a long road ahead, but at least there was a road. The pipe would go… well, smoking the pipe would go. He would keep an empty pipe hanging out of his mouth, because you can't be Russell Finn without a pipe. As soon as he was well enough, he was going to go right to Larry Edwards store and order one of those new respirator masks like Jack had. This had punished his wife something terrible, and he was going to make it right. He could feel himself getting rolled down the hallway back to his room. All those reporters were gone now. Melissa had held her own. "Say pop". He thought to himself. She had stolen that from him. He had said it to some blow boater once that had come too close while they were hauling. The asshole comment was something he had never heard before. She may have been hanging out with him and Clive too long. He couldn't wait to get this breathing tube out and get out of this… sleep. Dr. Cole had told him he would be coming out of the coma soon. She was different from other doctors. She talked to him and let him know what was going on, even though he couldn't say or do anything to respond. Soon he would be able to open his eyes, and see his family, hold his wife. He wouldn't be able to talk for a bit, Dr. Cole said, but he was okay with that. He had been given one hell of a scare. Now it was time to be thankful that it was just a scare.

Demetri Balfour had picked up his phone to call Paul for an update when his news app had sent him a notification. He had set up his news app to send him reports of any headlines involving Melissa Andrews. Sure enough, there was a reporter standing outside of Maine Medical Center, reporting how she had just been verbally abused by the retired actress. A video clip showed Melissa speaking to the reporter. The audio on the video was garbled except for what Melissa was saying was clear as day, "out of your ass" and "asshole." The reporter apologized for the garbled audio, saying there was a background noise issue. Demetri chuckled to himself. His target had not only revealed herself, but she was right here in Portland. "Ah… if only the timing was a little better," he said out loud to himself. He texted Paul to tell him that the person he was supposed to be tracking was right in Portland at Maine Med. His low-level contact in the FBI said that Agent Rand was being heavily watched. He could use that to his advantage if he had someone higher, like the late Agent Ross, on the inside. It would be best if the person was in charge of the investigation. His contact had told him it was Agent Roberts and gave him all of the agent's information. He stroked his chin and grinned. "One more piece set in motion," he said. Now for another piece; where to hold the auction for Agent Rand and Melissa Andrews. "A discrete location… hidden… mobile?... maybe…. yes, how perfect." He spoke to himself out loud. He turned to his computer and started searching for another yacht.

Chapter 8

Lucy Finn sat in her father's room and watched out the window as the sun went down over Hadlock Field. She looked over to her father, still sleeping away. Dr. Cole said it would take some time for him to wake up. Sam walked into the room with some carry-out from a local restaurant.

"Hey, do you mind going out to the nurse's station and asking for some napkins or paper towels? I forgot to grab some."

Lucy walked out, and just as the door closed, Sam saw them at the bottom of the bag. He turned to open the door to stop her when he saw a book in the corner. He picked it up and read the cover, and he got weak in the knees. "Pregnancy? Lucy is pregnant?" Sam had never felt so happy and terrified at the same time. He had been considering popping the question but was thinking about timing; as soon as he and Lucy were married, he wanted to start having kids. Why hadn't she told him? How long had she known? Maybe it was because of her father being in the hospital. Maybe she would tell him after Russell was awake or home. He could hear Lucy coming back, so he hid the book under a Commercial Fisheries News on the bedside table. After eating dinner, they fell asleep in their chairs.

Russell could hear a noise coming from the corner of his room. He focused his energy into opening his left eye. It slowly opened, but everything was dark and blurry. He then focused his energy on his right eye, and that slowly came open. He stared in the direction of the noise until his eyes were focused. It was Lucy, and she was snoring. He tried to speak, but his throat hurt too much. He wanted to wake her up and let her know he was awake. He looked around and saw the nurse's call button. He didn't want to make a fuss, but he was anxious to let Lucy know he was awake. He looked at his hand, three inches away from the button. He stared at his fingers, concentrating as hard as he could, until his index finger started to move. Then the other fingers slowly came online as well. Like a spider, he made his hand crawl to the remote. He slowly wrapped his hand around it and hit the red button with his thumb. Then the nurse came in and looked at Russell. He held his hand up, putting his finger and thumb together to make the "ok" signal. He then pointed to Lucy snoring in the corner. The nurse walked briskly to Lucy and placed a hand on her shoulder.

"Ms. Finn… Ms. Finn." The nurse said, with a gentle shake of Lucy's shoulder.

Lucy opened her eyes to see the nurse standing over her. Her heart jumped into her throat as she thought the worst, until she looked over and saw her father's open, and twinkling eyes and warm smile. "Daddy," she said as she went to his bedside and held his hand. The commotion had woken Sam up, and he went to Lucy's side. The nurse reminded them it would be a while before he could talk, and she was going to let Dr. Cole know he was awake. Lucy told Sam to text the family to share the news. The rest of the Finn clan arrived after driving from Boothbay Harbor. Russell looked around at his family and had a single tear roll down his cheek. He motioned to Anne to grab a notebook and pen. He wrote two words and held it up for Melissa to see. "Say pop," it said. Melissa smiled at him while he gave her a thumbs up. After visiting for a while, Anne decided to stay while the rest planned to meet at Portland Pie Company before heading back home. While Jack was walking through the lounge on the way to the elevator, he swore he saw the man who vomited on his boots the day before. He looked again, but didn't see him. He shook it off and kept walking. After breakfast, they figured they would head home until Russell was talking. On the drive home, Jack decided to bring up the subject of moving in.

"So, how soon can I move in?" Jack asked.

"How soon do you want to move in?"

"Um… Well, Michael has The Harbor covered along with Abigial. Lizzy and Josh will be headed down after school. Why not move some stuff today?"

"That is not a bad idea. You can start with your clothes and other daily things."

"I am thinking of leaving the furniture there. Rent it out as a furnished house. You can come look if you want anything for your place."

"Yeah, we may need your dresser."

"I want to get started on the baby's room too!"

"Hold on there, cowboy. Let's wait a little bit. We still have the doctor's appointment next week to confirm it, and we can't go tipping off people quite yet."

"OK, but as soon as it's announced, operation Baby Finn Nursery goes into effect."

"Are you sure about moving in? I mean, we, as usual, are taking some very big steps rather quickly."

"Well, the way I see it, we have a dog, we will soon be living together, then getting married, then having a baby. The baby will make us slow down!"

"Good point."

While her mother had left earlier to start dinner for them and their guest, Michael let Lizzy leave early too. He and Josh would lock up. By the time Josh and Michael came through the door, Lizzy was already out of the shower and dressed. Soon the kitchen smelled of Abigail's signature alfredo sauce and baked chicken topped with mayonnaise, breadcrumbs, and grated parmesan cheese. Lizzy was debating telling her family about Liam's stutter when the headlights from Liam's father's truck could be seen in the driveway. Michael looked at his wristwatch and nodded his head in approval.

Liam could see the family inside the house. He started getting nervous and considered getting back into the truck, but, almost as if his dad sensed it, his father backed out and left. He walked up onto the porch, then realized he was almost crushing the flowers he had gotten Lizzy's mother. He relaxed his grip on the flowers and took a larger than normal step to the door.

Lizzy eagerly waited on the other side of the door until she heard him knock. She opened the door so quickly that it startled Liam, and he dropped the flowers. They both bent over at the same time, bumping heads on the way down. Both of them looked red as fire trucks in their faces. Liam was so nervous now he couldn't breathe and didn't dare speak; that was until he saw Lizzy smile at him. He relaxed and took a breath.

"Don't just stand there, Lizzy; let the boy in," said Michael.

"Come in, Liam." Liam stepped inside timidly, and Lizzy closed the door. "Liam, this is my family. You already know Josh." Josh leaned in and gave him a firm handshake. "This is my dad, Mic...." Michael cut her off, "Mr. Williams," Michael said as he stuck out his hand. Liam put his hand in Michael's to give him a firm handshake. He was expecting it was going to be like shaking hands with a bench vice, but it wasn't. It was a good firm grip, like what his father had taught him.

"And this is my mom, Mrs. Williams."

"You can call me Abigail."

Now it was his turn to speak. He already knew he was going to stutter, there was no stopping it. Accepting it and going with it was the best way to handle it.

"T-T-T-T-The-these are for you, M M M Mrs. W-W-W-Wiliams."

In the same time that Abigail processed the fact Liam stuttered, she also decided to ignore it. "Thank you, Liam, I will put them in a vase right away. Everyone can sit down, and Lizzy and I will put food on the table."

Liam removed the Brooks Trap Mill baseball hat from his head and sat down. He chanced a look over at Michael and caught an approving look. He breathed a little deeper now, starting to relax.

"So, Liam, what's your plan after you get out of school?" Michael asked.

"He has applied to Texas A&M for engineering."

"Lizzy, let him answer, please. Engineering, huh. Any idea what field?"

"I-I-I-I eventually want to get into robotics, N-N-N-Not the software side but the h-h-hardware side." Liam paused for a moment, as if he had a sudden thought. "I-I-I forgot to say t-t-t-th-thank you for your service, M-M-Mr. Williams."

"It was a privilege, Liam. May I ask why you didn't choose the military?"

"I-I-I wanted to b-b-but m-m-my stutter."

Michael could see the mix of emotion in the young man before him. The kid was nervous, embarrassed, and now a bit disappointed. "That's too bad, it seems like they're losing a good man."

Abigail put the pasta, sauce, and chicken on the table while Lizzy set the garlic bread down. Then she set down a bowl of peas. Michael saw the change in expression on Liam's face as she set the peas down.

"Liam, those peas I grew right in our garden. I even canned them myself, I grew so much," Lizzy said.

Knowing that, and seeing how proud of the peas Lizzy was, he grabbed a big scoop of them. Then, filled his plate with the other items. He ate the peas first; he hated every spoonful but nobody at the table would have known. Liam seemed to stutter less and less as the night went on. After dessert and some more conversation, Michael offered to take Liam home. Liam and Michael got into the truck first, while Lizzy went to get a sweatshirt.

"You don't like peas, do ya?" Michael asked.

"No, not at all." Liam answered.

"I think you are pretty brave kid. Coming over for dinner, knowing you had a stutter. You must really like my daughter to eat peas and put yourself in a situation, where you would have to talk." Michael paused a bit and left a bit of an awkward silence. "I was going to tell you that while you two are on your date, to treat my daughter with respect. I was going to do the whole tough dad routine on you. I have been waiting all of Lizzy's life to do it, but you seem to be a good young man. I know she is driving but I will tell you what I am going to tell her. I want her home by 11:00. No funny business. Ok."

"Yes, sir"

"You can call me Michael."

Lizzy came out the front door, and Michael hopped out of the driver seat.

"Lizzy, you can drive him home in my truck. I am beat and want to get to bed. Don't stay out too late, it's a school night."

"Thank you, Daddy!"

<hr>

Friday morning, Russell was released from the hospital. Dr. Cole and some of the nurses escorted him out and gave him many hugs. The outside air felt good to Russell, but he wanted to smell the Boothbay Harbor air as soon as possible. When he got home, he found that Jack had moved out of his house. Anne had told him he and Melissa had been moving his stuff to her house, but the empty driveway and knowing that Jack's house was empty was a sting. He and Jack had built that house with help from a local contractor. It was time, though. Jack and Melissa needed room to grow. Anne helped him up the stairs into their own home. On the kitchen table was a brand-new pipe, but she had thrown out all the bags of pipe tobacco. He picked up the pipe and clenched it between his teeth as he always had. When he inhaled, through it, it was nothing but clean air, complimented with a subtle whistle. "Ha, that will take some getting used to," he said, out loud.

"Zeke's funeral is tomorrow. I already told his daughter you may not be there-"Anne started to say before Russell cut her off.

"Why would you tell her that? Zeke was a friend of mine, and he fished for me. Ain't no way in hell I am missing that funeral."

"Ok, Russell, I just figured being…you know… That a funeral would be the last place you would want to be."

"That little stint in the hospital taught me a lot. You know I was able to hear all of you. I had to hear all the pain my stubbornness had created. Anne, we have our first grandchild on the way. Our son is going to be getting married, and I think our daughter is not far behind, given what Sam was saying, when I was in the coma. I am going to that funeral, and I am going to be thankful that I am there and on the other side of the grass."

"Alright then, I will get your suit out and get it ready. Clive has organized Zeke's boat parade for after the funeral, Zeke's daughter and her family are going to watch from the dock. As she said, they are not boating people. Then we will all meet up at The Harbor for a reception."

"Can you imagine that, Anne. I remember that little girl always being on the boat. When Patricia died, everything went south. She was what held that family together. Poor ole' Zeke died, hardly knowing his grandkids. To think I got all wound up over Jack moving just down the road."

"That is all behind us now. You just need to worry about following Dr. Cole's orders. You got to take it easy for a while, Russell, and don't you dare let me catch you with any tobacco in that pipe!"

Russell snapped to attention and gave Anne a mock salute. To which she rolled her eyes and scoffed, "Ox!".

⁓⁕⁘⁖⁗⁙⁖⁘⁕⁓

Jack and Melissa were working at the lobster retail side of The Harbor. Another bait truck had come, and Melissa was running the fork truck, unloading the truck. Jarvis was never far away, but never underfoot. Melissa had put the last tote in the bait shed and parked the fork truck when she noticed a man waiting to get some lobster. He had a black baseball hat, glasses, and a mask.

"Can I help you, sir?"

"Yes, could I get two pound and a quarter lobsters and a small container of scallops."

"Sure thing, are you traveling far? If so, I can pack them in a couple of ice packs. It will be another ten dollars."

"No, I am staying close by. Do you mind me asking… are you really the Melissa Andrews?

"That depends… if you are a reporter asking me about harassing reporters at the hospital, you can get lost."

"Nope, I am a fan of yours; always have been."

"Ok, then, in that case, I will sign one of our post cards for you for free."

Jack had just walked in at this point and put his hands on her hips gently while stepping around her. The man noticed her smile grew a little with Jack's gentle touch. These two were very much the couple the media reported them to be.

"Sir, that will be $45.83."

He pulled out cash from a pocket and paid Melissa. The gentleman seemed to be pre-occupied with what Jack was doing. When Jack walked back out, he turned to Melissa, took a longer than normal pause and said thank you, and walked out. Melissa thought nothing of it and went back to her duties.

Jack had finished up business with a boat on the dock and noticed the man watching over the harbor. He couldn't really tell if he was watching Jack or just the general direction. Jack decided to walk up and greet him.

"Can I help you, sir?" Jack asked.

"You must be Jack."

"Yes, I must be. May I ask who you are?"

By this time, Jack had closed the distance between them.

"I am just a fan of you both," said the man, while taking off his shaded glasses. He looked up at Jack, looked right at Jack's face. Jack saw the man's eyes, and they looked familiar. "You have a great girl; Jack, take good care of her." The man turned and walked away.

Chapter 9

Melissa had been to a few funerals in her life, even her own mother's. This was different, though. This one was the first in her newfound life. There were many of the fellow lobstermen there; they looked much different to Melissa, all dressed up and looking so serious. Russell looked sharp in his suit, as old men often do. He walked arm in arm with Anne. They sat down next to Zeke's daughter, who had her husband and their two children beside them. She didn't even know Zeke had grandkids. The whole family looked on stoically. It occurred to Melissa that the lobstermen standing up behind the chairs knew Zeke more than his family sitting in them. Even Jarvis seemed to show more emotion than Zeke's family. After the funeral was over, everyone headed to their boats to get ready for the boat parade in Zeke's honor.

"Hollywood, would you mind runnin' *Old Smoke* for me?" asked Russell, to which Melissa nodded in agreement.

The sky was gray and overcast, the air was chilly, and the harbor was spotted with boats ready to start lining up. Zeke's boat was tied up at the outer most float at The Harbor. Anne had gotten a picture of Zeke, placed it in a wreath, and had it out on the transom of the boat. She would stand with Zeke's family on the dock. Russell had a chair set up in *Old Smoke* for him to sit down in. They headed up the line, while the other boats fell in behind. Melissa kept the boat slow and steady, just a couple hundred RPMs above idle. Jarvis had jumped up onto the wash rail and got up on the bow of the boat. He sat down but kept his nose high in the air. They came in through the harbor nice and slow, tucking inside of Harbor Island and going past the Tugboat Inn. As Melissa made the turn by the Footbridge, she looked back at the line of boats still passing Harbor Island. Russell sat in his chair, empty pipe in his mouth, and a distant stare. Melissa faced forward again, looking out the windshield of the boat. Jarvis remained on the bow, head held high. "Does he know what is going on?" Melissa asked herself.

Russell sat looking at the boats and the ocean, thinking that they almost had a boat parade for him. He felt an odd mix of relief and sadness. A long breath helped him settle a bit. Zeke was gone. There would be no more waves as he walked by the window in the morning. No more helping him get his bait aboard the boat. But he would have a chance to keep living, to see his kids get married, and watch his grandchildren grow. A single tear rolled down his cheek.

Melissa looked back to Russell, about to ask something, but then saw the tear and decided not to. They were heading to Zeke's boat now. She could see Anne standing next to Zeke's family. She turned the boat a bit to get as close as she could, then turned the other way. Just as she did this, Jarvis let out two loud barks as if to say goodbye. Now Melissa had a couple tears running down her cheeks. She left the wheel to wave at the family, then turned toward the middle of the Harbor.

"Hollywood, this is when you hit the throttle!"

Melissa shrugged and told Jarvis to lay down. She eased the throttle up to full throttle; as soon as she got to full throttle, the *Red At Night* passed on her starboard and *Overtime* passed on the port. The *Old Smoke* pitched and rolled with the other boats wake and Russell started yelling about getting rolled upside down. Melissa laughed at him while watching his chair slide around on deck. They tied up at The Harbor, shared stories about Zeke, and raised their drinks in a final salute.

In a deep contrast to the dark, cold, dreary day Saturday was, Sunday came and the sun was beaming and not a cloud in the sky. It actually felt warm out for a change. Everyone was ready for a Finn Family breakfast. The Williams were there, and with Lizzy and Abigail in the kitchen with Lucy and Melissa, Anne sat back and helped when needed. The conversion was focused on Lizzy's first date with Liam. Lizzy blushed a bit at first, then they all started talking about their first dates.

"Mom, do you remember Chris Thatcher? I thought dad was going to throw him out the window!"

"What did he do?" asked Lizzy

"He didn't remove his hat when sitting at the table, then when Russell prompted him to do so, he said he didn't have to. Russell asked him to either leave the table or Russell would make him leave." said Anne.

"He took one look at dad, then got up and left. Jack took his plate." Added Lucy.

Breakfast hit the table, and everyone sat and ate. As usual, Jack and Michael got up for seconds and thirds. Then, the talk of highs and lows of the week, along with goals set for the following week. Jack, Michael, Josh, and Sam started clearing the table, while Lizzy, Abigail, and Anne walked outside for Anne to show her plan for the garden. Russell was allowed to skip the kitchen duties for this week and sat down in a lawn chair to listen to the garden plan. Instead of going out to the gardens, Melissa took a chair next to Russell.

"You gave me a bit of a scare last week,old timer." Melissa paused a bit to think about how to word her next sentence. "I am not trying to take Jack away from you. I…"

Russell lifted his hand to pause Melissa. "I understand; I am sorry I acted the way I did. I was worried about how much time I had left, and I have had both my kids right here, all my life. Now, it's so quiet without Jack here, I may just kick Lucy and Sam out!" He stopped to see Melissa smile. "I get it, Hollywood; you need to prove to yourself you can handle it. Anne and I already know you two are going to be great parents."

Melissa grabbed Russell's hand and gave it a squeeze. "Now I have to ask you for a favor. Would you mind giving me away at the wedding?"

"You mean taking place as your father… It would be a privilege." Said Russell, beaming with pride.

Melissa gave Russell a big hug.

"Now, I have a question for you. Will you be my sternwoman for the trap hauling contest?"

"Trap hauling contest? What is that?"

"Christ, Jack ain't told you about the Fishermen's Festival?!"

"No, what is it?"

"It's usually the last weekend in April, so the kids can get their skiffs together and have time to practice during April vacation. On Friday is the Miss Shrimp Pageant. Girls ages 9 to 12 show their talents. Some sing, some dance, some play an instrument. Lucy came in runner up one year juggling, and Lizzy got the crown her first year doing jump ropes! Saturday morning starts off with a pancake breakfast put on by the Lions Club at 6:00 AM. The fun really starts at 8:00 AM with the Cod Fish Relay Race. All four classes from the high school select 4 runners. Each runner has to put on all foul weather gear, including boots, and carry two codfish around the downtown loop. After that, it's the bait shoveling contest. You dump a barrel of bait and fill three trays. After that, there is the crate running, then dory bailing. Then it's time for my favorite, the trap hauling contest. There are two separate races. The skiff fishermen and the big boats. The skiff fishermen are broken up into three groups, middle school, high school, and adult. They run from the top of the ramp, jump in their boat, go haul a single trap, set it back, then come back to the dock. The big boats do the same thing, but they haul a complete string of five traps. That pretty much wraps up the waterfront stuff. Then we go up to the elementary school for scallop shucking, shrimp picking, net mending and lobster eating. Ole Stevie Hodgdon has the record for that one at 1 minute and 54 seconds, but I suppose Josh may take it this year. Saturday night is the tall tale's competition at Brady's, where us old guys tell fish tales. Jennie Mitchell ends up clearing the floor for dancing afterwards. Sunday is a bit more somber as a priest from the Catholic Church comes out and reads off the names of those lost at sea from the area. Then comes the blessing of the fleet, where we all circle around, like we did for Zeke, and come by the dock, and the priest blesses our boats."

"Wow, that sounds like fun. Can I enter any of these? Like the bait shoveling and the lobster eating?"

"Sure, but will you do the trap hauling competition?"

"Hell Yes!"

"That's my Hollywood!"

"Is there any way I can help?"

"Corey Pottle and Ryan Casey took it over after Clive and I retired from it, they will be having a meeting at Kaler's this week. I will find out when and let them know you are coming."

"What are you two talking about ?" asked Anne.

"Hollywood is going to go with me for the trap hauling contest."

"And I am going to do the bait shoveling and lobster eating contest!"

"Picture that, Melissa Andrews picking and eating two lobsters as fast as she can." Said Lucy

"Oh… I didn't think of that. You know the media will be all over it. Maybe I should just stick to the trap hauling."

"No way, I mean, it's up to you, of course, but, it would draw a crowd and help to raise money."

Jack, Sam, Michael, and Josh had finished the dishes and cleaning the kitchen and joined them in the conversation.

"Josh, you want to do the trap hauling with me?" Jack asked.

"I don't know; I am already doing the cod fish race, bait shoveling, crate running, and doing the skiff trap hauling. My arms are going to be noodles." Josh replied.

"What about you, Lizzy?"

"The same, except I am doing the dory bailing with Hazel, not the trap hauling."

"Well, I can ask Justin Lewis or Butch Brewer. They are fast too."

Jack lurched forward, almost knocked off his feet. He looked beside him, and Michael was grinning. "What about me? I will do trap hauling with you."

"Ok, but we need to practice. Every year, Corey and Ryan go together, and they take first place; last year, they set the record. I am gunning for them this year, after a 5-year break."

While the group talked more about the Fisherman's Festival, Lizzy pulled Jack, Melissa, and Sam aside.

"Hey, we need at least four chaperones for the prom this year, and the students really don't want teachers or parents. We are looking for younger people who will be able to blend in better. Would you guys be willing to do it? We do ask that you dress up for it; you know, dresses and tuxes. The teachers also want us to have at least one law enforcement officer, so I will be asking Agent Rand."

"Could Lucy come too? I am sure she would love to help, and more adults would be better." asked Sam.

"I am sure there would be no problem with that. There is possibly going to be over one hundred students there."

Both Jack and Melissa nodded at each other and agreed.

"Great, I am going to give Agent Rand a call this afternoon, and that will be all set. Thanks guys!"

Sam started thinking to himself. "That will be perfect...after all the kids leave, I could take Lucy out on to the dance floor and ask her to marry me. I already bought the ring."

Lizzy walked to her father and spoke. "I helped your plan along a little. Both Jack and Melissa are going to be chaperones for prom. They will be dressed up and everything. I will get them to go to the dance floor after all the students leave."

"Nice, good girl. That should work out perfectly!"

Later that evening, Lizzy called Agent Rand, to ask her about chaperoning.

"Hi Agent Rand, how are you?"

Agent Rand was so tired of people asking that. She was a prisoner in her own home; sure, she could leave ,but there would be agents following her the whole time. Her phone was being monitored, her house was wired, she was a suspected felon, and she was on suspension. She knew that Lizzy had no idea what was going on at the moment.

"I am doing all right Lizzy, you know you can call me Carla, right. You are not a probie yet."

"I know, I know, as soon as I am a probationary officer, I have to call you Agent Rand, get you coffee, and bagels, and clean your car."

"You will have to call me Agent Rand; all that other stuff you don't have to worry about…. unless I am assigned as your training officer, then remember, I like my coffee with two sugars, no creamer, everything bagel with veggie cream cheese. "

"Got it, hey I want to ask you a favor. My prom is coming up in May, and my teachers want to have at least one law enforcement officer as a chaperone. Would you mind chaperoning?"

Carla Rand was stuck; she technically was still an agent, but on suspension. Her phone beeped with an incoming text message from Andy.

I am on duty and listening in. Ask if you can bring a guest. I will go with you, and that will keep the brass happy.

Carla rolled her eyes at the invasion of privacy but was glad she had a solution.

"Lizzy, can I bring a guest with me? He is another agent."

"Sure Agent Rand, you do have to dress up. We want the chaperones to blend in."

"Lizzy, you know how I hate dresses, but for you it's a done deal. Just remember this when you are getting my coffee and bagel."

"Thank you, Agent Rand. I will text you more details when we have more of a plan."

"Okay, Lizzy, talk to you later."

As much as Carla Rand hated wearing dresses and dressing up, she actually was looking forward to this.

Monday afternoon, Jack was in the dock house again, painting buoys and getting traps ready, when Sam came barging through the door. Jack looked up to see Sam as pale as a ghost, his eyes welling up. "Sam, you alright?" Jack asked while turning down the radio.

"Is Lucy pregnant?"

The question shocked Jack. Why would Sam be asking him if Lucy was pregnant. He had forgotten all about running into Alyssa at Walmart. He tried to talk, but Sam cut him off.

"I found a pregnancy book in Russell's hospital room the night when Lucy and I were up there, and now I just saw Alyssa Allen in Hannaford, and she said she saw you and Melissa in the baby section at Walmart. She said you were shopping for Lucy. Is she pregnant? Why hasn't she told me? Am I the father?"

Jack had a flashback to running into Alyssa; he plopped the paint brush he was holding into the paint can so hard, some of it splashed up. He grabbed a rag and wiped his hands, grabbed a couple of the Footbridge Brewery beers he had in the fridge, and passed one to Sam. This seemed to make Sam more concerned, so he decided to get right to it.

"Melissa is pregnant. She and I were looking at baby stuff at Walmart when Alyssa saw us, and we needed to explain it. So, I said Lucy was pregnant. Melissa got that book from a lady in the maternity ward, while she was watching over Dad." Jack said, then took an extended sip from his beer.

Sam leaned back in his chair and let the feeling of relief wash over him. He then took a long sip of beer and leaned forward to Jack. "Lucy is going to kill you if this gets out, I mean, it's already kinda out. Not that Alyssa is a busy body, but it's going to get out. What happens if she runs into Lucy?"

"Well, I think the four of us need to talk. Melissa isn't going to be happy, she wanted to wait a while before telling everyone."

"Lucy is at the Harbor for another couple of hours."

"Melissa is up at the school helping with that play. I will text her to come down to The Harbor when done."

"Well, Congratulations."

"Thanks Sam,"

Jack texted Melissa while he and Sam finished their beers. Both were really not looking forward to what was coming next. When they got to The Harbor, Lucy was wiping down tables and cleaning up. Melissa had just parked her car and was walking in behind them. Lucy looked up and tensed up.

"Is dad, ok?"

"Yes, Dad is ok; the four of us need to have a little talk," said Jack, not knowing where to start. This was such a mess, and he didn't know how he wanted to announce it.

"Melissa, remember the other night when we were at Walmart and got…. caught… in that section?

Melissa had to think for a second, "yeah…" she said while cocking her head to the side, wondering where this was going.

"Lucy, we were in Walmart the other night, and Alyssa Allen saw us in the baby section. When she asked why we were there, I said you were pregnant."

"Pregnant! We are not even married! Do you think I am stupid enough to get knocked up." Lucy yelled.

Jack looked over at Melissa, who was now flush with embarrassment. Lucy caught the look and immediately regretted what she had just said. Jack and Melissa were in Walmart, looking at baby stuff, not too long after announcing they were getting married, and Jack was now moving in with Melissa. There was a moment of silence while they tried to figure out what to say.

"Melissa, I didn't mean it like that. I was angry." She glanced at Jack. "Very angry, but I understand why you didn't want the news out. I don't think you are stupid, and I am happy for you." Lucy took a deep breath. "And I am willing to keep up the charade that I am pregnant if you guys need a cover, but I am doing it for you, not my chowdah head brother."

Melissa let a chuckle out. "No, it's only a matter of time before people start to find out. We certainly didn't plan this, and I didn't ask him to marry me because of it. I had been planning on asking him for weeks. I still have to go see the doctor before it's officially official."

"I am sorry, Lucy; I could have said we were shopping for a friend; I just didn't think. This was certainly not the way I wanted you to find out, either. We were just waiting a couple months before we made the big announcement."

"Do Mom and Dad know?"

"Yes, but that is it. I haven't told Michael or anyone else."

"Well, congratulations to you two! I am going to be an aunt! Aunt Lucy has a ring to it!"

"Great... I am going to be the government...," said Sam.

"What?!" said Jack.

"Uncle Sam..."

"You are not going to be an uncle anything if you don't hurry up and put a ring on my finger," said Lucy in a half joking, half jeering tone. It was enough to break the tension.

Soon it was the day for the appointment with the doctor. Jack and Melissa borrowed Abigail's car, to shake the media. Jack pulled into the parking lot and turned off the car.

"So, what do you think the doctor is going to say?" Jack asked.

"I am pretty sure she is going to say I am pregnant." Melissa responded.

"You are still sure?"

"Oh yeah, I did another test, and my friend hasn't visited for the month."

"Eeww...."

"Oh Jack, you are about to learn more about my anatomy in the next 9 months than you ever wanted to know."

"I know, I know. I am ready."

"I know you are. Today they are just drawing blood, and it will take a couple days before they give us the results. We will also talk about the planning of appointments, a general screening of both our medical histories, basically an ice breaker."

"Well then, let's go in and break some ice!"

Melissa and Jack marched into the doctor's office, holding hands. Nervous, apprehensive, but strong.

The time passed by quickly. Paul kept his tabs on Melissa's location. He had her schedule down and knew when and where to find her. The media made that task easy. Even though she had retired from acting, some of the paparazzi still liked to track her. Paul's other associate kept tabs on Agent Rand. Demetri Balfore was working on organizing the auction for Melissa and Agent Rand. He had bought a new yacht and had sent out invitations of sorts to several clients. The auction had a $250,000 buy in just to get on the boat. All communication was coded, and identities put under strict scrutiny so no undercover agents would slip through. Balfour's operation was airtight. He just had to wait to hear back from all invited guests before he could set a date. The yacht had a helicopter pad and a small but fast center console boat; this would help the customers leave the yacht easily. After all the customers had left, he would set the autopilot for a crash course into The Harbor, with enough explosives onboard to remove it from the coastline. The distraction would be enough to tie up local enforcement for days. All he had to do was be patient.

Melissa was working at the school, then practicing with Russell. She had joined the Fisherman's Festival Committee helping Heather Casey, Ryan's wife, with the pageant, though Melissa thought Heather had it well under control. She had managed to track down the dress that Michael had wanted to get and was working with Abigail to get it fit for Lizzy, without Lizzy knowing. Russell spent the time mostly sitting and recovering, either sitting at home reading the Register or sitting at The Harbor manning one of the cash registers. He and Anne had started walking once a day and had worked up to twice a day.

Chapter 10

Fisherman's Festival weekend had arrived, and it was Friday night. Jack was sitting on the bed in his best blue jeans and flannel while Melissa scurried about in a dark purple dress, finishing her hair and make-up while trying to put in earrings.

"Jack, how do these earrings look with this dress?"

"I don't know; I am thinking about taking that dress off right now."

"Jack, not now; I am trying to get ready. All that fooling around is what got us in this situation anyway."

"Well, I like this situation, so, let's fool around some more!"

"No, I need to get there early. Heather tasked me with helping the girls before they get on stage. You know, pep talks and stuff. I have to be there for those girls."

"Well then, the white pearl earrings look the best, your hair and make-up look great. Now quit fussing, and let's get going."

"Did you feed Jarvis?"

"Jarvis is fed; he has been out and is laying on the couch half asleep."

The pageant was held at the elementary school gymnasium, but was decorated in such a way so the contestants felt like they were on Broadway. Hundreds of folding chairs were laid out, many of them reserved for the families of the contestants. Jack joined his family in the back row of chairs while Melissa hurried off backstage.

"Where is Hollywood?" asked Russell.

"She went backstage to help the girls get ready. She is taking this pretty seriously; she loves those kids."

The lights in the gymnasium dimmed, and the few clattering footsteps climbing up the old wooden bleachers were soon drowned out by the MC, Mark Gimbel's signature voice. He made the intro and had last year's Miss Shrimp pageant winner, Amy Grant, come out and greet the crowd. After a quick speech by Amy, the contestants started with their performances. One girl did a stand-up comedy bit, another sang "Imagine". There was some piano and guitar playing, and a juggling act.

"Next up is Michelle Hyson, singing Mary Chapin Carpenter's "Down at the Twist and Shout".

"Ok, Michelle, it's your turn." Melissa said, while gesturing for Michelle to get on stage.

"I can't. I can't do it. There are way too many people out there," said Michelle, starting to cry.

"Michelle, I heard you sing last night at the rehearsal. You are too good to not do this. Listen, just close your eyes; I will walk you out to the stage and put the mic in your hand. Then just start singing. Before you know it, you will be opening your eyes and dancing around the stage. Now let's do this."

Melissa took Michelle's hand and walked her out on stage. She placed the mic in her hand and stood there with her hand on her back while the music started. On que, Michelle started to sing.

"Saturday night and the moon is out...."

She kept on singing, and the crowd started clapping with the beat. Michelle opened her eyes and started bouncing a bit with the beat. The bouncing turned into dancing, and the crowd kept clapping. At the end of the song, there was a standing ovation. Michelle bowed and calmly walked off the stage.

"Wow, what a show! Let's have these ladies come up for one more round of applause!" The girls came up and bowed once more, and stood on stage. "I would like to take this moment to introduce our judges from right to left, and please stand when I say your name; we have John Farnham, Sally Luke, Louise Doty, Gerald Hyson, and Carol Brown. We will have a highlight reel of last year's show while the judges make their final decision."

A highlight reel played while some stood to stretch.

"The judges have narrowed the selection down to three contestants. May I get Emily Trudo, Michelle Hyson, and Nicole Smith on stage, please."

The three girls walked on stage and held hands.

"The second runner up is Nichole Smith!" The crowd cheered while Nicole accepted the runner up sash.

"The winner of this year's Miss Shrimp Pageant is…." A drum roll started while Mark unfolded the winner's name. "Michelle Hyson!"

The crowd cheered with excitement while the tiara and sash were placed on Michelle. Melissa came out and gave her a big hug.

Jack caught up with Melissa outside of the backstage area and headed home. Tomorrow was going to be a big day, and they wanted to get to bed.

The next morning, after a good breakfast of pancakes, the Williams and Finn crowd found a good spot to watch the codfish race. Liam Deene joined them as well, standing next to Lizzy. Corey Pottle and Ryan Casey were telling the crowd about the event briefly before the start. Lizzy's best friend, Hazel, would be running first for the seniors. Both the Williams kids had decided not to run in the codfish race so they could save their energy for other events. The participants all took their positions to get ready to put all the gear on the first runner.

"On your mark…get set…" All could see the tension building in the runners. "Hey Ryan, did I tell you I found a string of yours hung down on the north end of Squirrel Island?" Corey said to confuse the runners.

"No, you didn't, but thanks for telling, GO!" Ryan yelled.

They hurried about first putting on the bib overalls known as "oil skins", then the team members stood the first runner up and while two of them helped put on boots, the other put on the foul weather jacket and helped with gloves. Once the boots were on, the other two put big cod fish in each of the runners' hands, and the runner took off.

"And there they go around the corner and up Boothbay House Hill Rd. That hill is much steeper when you are wearing all that gear and carrying two cod fish!" said Corey.

"Looks like Hazel is pulling ahead while turning the corner on to McKown St." Ryan shouted into the microphone.

"That Hazel Westin runs like a scared cat!" Said Russell.

As the rest of the runners rounded the corner, they went out of sight while running down McKown St., Hazel growing the seniors lead as she rounded the corner by Sherman's Bookstore with its staff out cheering.

"Now here is the tough part; runnin' down that hill can be just as bad as the run up the other one. You have to downshift a bit, or you will end up ass over band box!" said Corey.

Hazel made it to the start area first, and her team strategically removed her gear and put it on the next runner. The other teams repeated this. In the end, the lead that Hazel got was enough to keep the win for the seniors. The sophomores came in second, freshmen third, leaving the juniors last and having to clean up after the event.

"Next event is the bait shoveling contest. Each contestant will dump a barrel of bait. Then shovel it into 3 trays. Once you are done shoveling, you need to put both hands in the air and yell, "Done!" We have 6 contestants this year. First is Lizzy Williams, who shovels bait down at The Harbor; you're gonna wanta watch her. I know she is fast. Then we have her little brother, Josh. Next, we have Everett

Trask, Hugh Tompson, Jack Finn, and his newly announced fiancé, Melissa Andrews!" Corey boomed.

"Hold on, Corey, are you telling me we have a sibling rivalry, a future marriage, and a movie star all in this event? Christ, you can't make this up, folks!" Ryan jested, "Alright shovelers, grab a shovel, stand by a barrel, and lay out your trays."

Melissa grabbed a bait shovel, then placed all three of her trays on their side in a half-moon shape, with the opening towards the barrel. Then, she took a place behind the barrel. Jack looked slightly confused, but before he could ask or comment, Corey said "Go!"

All six contestants body checked their barrels of bait to knock them over. Jack looked over at Melissa to see that her bait barrel had tipped over and had sent a couple shovels full of bait into the trays she had tipped on their side. Ryan made a comment about Melissa being the brains in the operation. Melissa now pitched the bait directly into each tray, getting them as full as she could while on their side. She quickly tipped them up right and used the half full trays as a backstop to shovel against. She could see that Jack had one full and was close to filling another. Everett had stolen Hugh's bait shovel and tossed it, while Hugh had dumped out one of Everett's trays of bait. Josh and Lizzy seemed to be tied at about a tray and a half each. Melissa gritted her teeth and put every effort into what she was doing. She forgot about Jack and the others. She ignored her arms feeling like spaghetti. She filled the last tray and threw her hands up, accidentally tossing the bait shovel.

"We have a winner!" Corey yelled.

"And Jack in second!" Ryan announced two seconds later.

They all watched as Josh and Lizzy went shovel full to shovel full, but in the end, Josh had won by a pogie. The brother and sister shook hands. Everett had managed to put his bait barrel over Hugh's head and was drumming on the sides of it.

Dory bailing was next. Melissa watched as Hazel and Lizzy stepped into a dory that had been filled halfway with water. After the start, the two girls bailed water out of their dory. First with 5-gallon buckets, then with Clorox jugs that had been cut. Once all the water was out, or enough to make the judges happy, the timers would record the time. Lizzy and Hazel took first place in that event. Crate running was always a crowd favorite, kids and adults running across a string of crates going from dock to dock. You could tell by the expression on their faces when they fell off or sunk the crates just how cold the water was. Though Josh was known to be quick on his feet, he had grown a little more than previous years and found himself knee high in the cold water, eventually succumbing and falling off the crates. Then came the events everyone had been waiting for: the skiff hauling contest and big boat trap hauling contest. Tony Williams, a cousin to the Williams family, was first to go, followed by Tylar Michaud. Then it was Josh's turn. The race official took a seat in Josh's skiff, *Tip Jar*. Josh had an electric hauler but was not allowed to use it for this. All traps had to be hand hauled. Josh had his Scania hat turned backwards and was in a running start position at the start of the ramp. For this event, they used a foghorn. The horn blasted, and Josh rocketed down the ramp.

"Christ, he doesn't run that fast for dinnah!" Michael yelled over the cheering crowd.

Josh jumped in his boat and started outboard. He quickly untied the bow and stern lines. He put the boat in gear and hit full throttle. As the skiff shot off, the race official fell out of his seat; Josh didn't seem to give it a moment's notice and steered directly to the first buoy. Once the buoy was alongside, he decided to throttle down, grab the buoy, but turn the boat hard to starboard rather than trying to back down. This way, the boat would come around for him. It worked. He was able to hold on to the rope and start pulling up the trap. He pulled as hard as he could, getting the 3-foot trap up and out of the water. He quickly opened the door, removed the old bait bag, and put a new one in, and closed the door. When he looked up, his plan had almost worked; his boat had turned just a little too far. He dumped the trap back over and took off back to the dock. He kept the throttle wide open until his bow passed the dock, then slowed down. He hit reverse, and his outboard backed down angrily. He quickly tied the bow and stern lines and ran back up the ramp. There was a loud cheer as he crossed the finish line. The timers recorded the time, then it was Sean Keeting's turn, followed by Rick Burnham.

"All right, in third place we have Tony Williams and his boat *Seven*. In second place, we have Josh Williams in his boat *Tip Jar*, and the winner of the trap hauling contest is Tylar Michaud!" Ryan announced. All the contestants shook hands and congratulated each other.

Melissa had bought the Fisherman's Festival committee a large outdoor LCD TV, a camera, and all the hardware to live stream from the camera. That way, the people on shore could see what happened inside the boats during the competition. A cameraman and an official would be on each of the boats but had to stay out of the way.

Russell got *Old Smoke* into position. Given that Russell was just in the hospital, they allowed him to stay in the boat. Melissa would have to run down the ramp, untie both the bow and stern line. Same when they came back in. Melissa would have to tie both lines and run back up the ramp. Normally, both the captain and the sternman make the run up and down the dock, and the captain can untie and tie one line.

Lizzy had helped Melissa braid her hair in twin braids. She had put a little eye black under her eyes for sport. There was no denying, she meant business. Russell had already told her they probably wouldn't make third place because the other people had faster boats. She didn't care. Today meant much more to her than that. Today, the bait shoveling contest, the trap hauling contest, and the lobster eating contest meant more to her than placement. She wanted to prove she belonged here. No, she would never be considered a "Mainah" as they said. She didn't care about that. She wanted to earn the respect of the men and women of the lobstering community. That meant more to her than all the movies, Grammys, Emmys, and lobster trophies. She was crouched down in a track start, she had a little bounce, and her arms were swinging. Corey was about to ask her if she was ready, but he could tell she was.

"On your mark, get set," There was a long pause, and Melissa half expected either Ryan or Corey to make some Hollywood joke. "Go!" Ryan yelled.

She sprinted down the ramp, paying close attention to the transition between the ramp and dock. One time during practice, she stumbled on the transition and face planted on the dock. Russell had called to her, "You can't go laying around during the trap hauling!". The memory put a smile on her face while she ran down the dock. Russell had remembered to wet the dock down. As she approached the boat, she dropped down to a slide like a baseball runner sliding into home. Her eye locked on to the rope tying the bow of the boat to the dock, and she grabbed it and used her momentum to help untie it. She got up quickly, and untied the stern line, and yelled "Go." to Russell. She braced herself while the 210 Cummins turned up to 2600 RPMs. She made her way up towards Russell and grabbed the extra gaffe. She was to be back up in case Russell missed. He didn't; Russell grabbed the buoy and ran the rope up over the snatch block and around the hauler. Russell kept an eye on the bow and made sure they were heading along with the string. Up came the first trap, and Russell pulled it onto the rail. Melissa untied the bait line and opened the door. She had 5 bait irons set, each with an individual bag. She baited the trap, tossing the bait iron back, almost spearing the cameraman that got a little too close; the crowd on shore gasped. Melissa gave the camera man a nod to move back, then turned back to the trap, and closed the door, and gave the trap a spin while sliding the trap to the stern. She dashed back up to catch the second trap and repeated her steps, then the third, then the fourth, then the last she left on the rail for Russell to push when ready.

Just as she had practiced, she got out of the way during the setting back so not to get tangled in the ropes. The 210 Cummins came to full throttle again while setting back the traps. After all the traps and rope were off the boat, she took her position at the rail. Russell made the turn by the front of the dock, placing *Old Smoke* inches from it. Once at the foot of the ramp, Russell throttled down, placed the boat in reverse, then nailed the throttle again to get the boat to stop. Melissa jumped out, tied the stern line, then tied the bow line. She took off up the ramp; as she made her way up the ramp, she could hear Russell cheering, "Go Hollywood!" She reached the top of the ramp and raised her hands in triumph. The crowd cheered loudly as she caught her breath.

"You have to be one of the fastest stern…people I have ever met. Me and Corey have to run next, and I have to tell you, I wished I had asked you to go with me over Corey," said Ryan

Corey waited for the crowd to settle a bit. "Now, Melissa, we have to ask you a favor. Ryan and I are about to run, so we need someone to take over; would you mind taking the microphone for a bit? That is, if you are comfortable talking in large crowds?"

Melissa caught her breath a bit before answering. "I think I can handle it." She took the microphone and cleared her throat a bit. "All right, Boothbay Harbor, next up for the trap hauling competition is Ryan Casey in the *Harper Lee* with sternman Corey Pottle. They are defending their title as the fastest on the water. Are you guys ready!" They both gave a nod. "On your mark, get set… GO!" They both took off down the ramp and down the dock. Corey did a slide, similar to Melissa's, while Ryan got the boat started, then untied his line. Melissa gave a play-by-play while the big screen showed the onboard cameraman filming in real time. The crowd watched as the traps came up, were tended to, then put on the stern to set back. They were making good time. They set back the string, and zipped back to the dock, tied up, and ran up the ramp.

Fred Farnham, with his son Jerry, ran next in Fred's boat, the *Shellene Too*, followed by Paul Fasolo with his sternman, Keith Jordan, in Paul's boat, *Woody*. Keith had too much speed going into the slide and had slid right off the end of the dock. He had to scramble back on the dock and onboard. He did the whole race with water still in his boots. Then the last run would be Jack and Michael. Abigail mentioned that this had been something Michael had been wanting to do for a while. Back when Jack used to run it, he took Stephanie with him. Jack really wanted to win it this year. Michael stood there listening to Ryan, Corey, and now Melissa, who had joined them MCing. "Josh can run *Overtime* next year." he said to himself, but loud enough for Jack to hear.

"What?" asked Jack.

"She is way faster than me, Jack; you want to beat Corey and Ryan, you need to take her."

Before Melissa or Jack could argue, Michael took off his old black Scania hat and placed it backwards on Melissa's head. He was going to say something, but there were no words for the moment. A simple race in a small town that, in the grand scheme of things, may be trivial, but in this moment, meant the world to a 30-year-old

Hollywood actress who wanted to prove she had salt in her veins.

"Alright folks, we have a last-minute crew change here. We saw how fast she was for Russell. Let's see if she can do it again." said Ryan.

"Hey, you run faster than me, so you head down first and untie the bow line, I will get the stern. We will have to be careful as we cross each other when I go to start the boat."

"Ok, Jack."

Corey began the start. "On your mark, get set."

All sounds seemed to stop for Melissa except Corey's voice. She could see people cheering, but it looked as if they were in slow motion. She leaned down a little more and could feel Jack's hand on her shoulder. She drew in one big breath in anticipation.

"GO!" Corey yelled.

She took off down the ramp that shook a bit with every step Jack made. She locked her eyes on the rope tied just behind the davit and knew the dock was a little more slippery than before. She had no idea where Jack was now. She dropped into a slide and caught the rope. She saw Jack jump in the boat to untie the stern line. She watched him carefully as she untied her line and jumped into the boat. She hopped up on to the engine box to stay out of the way. Jack was still untying the stern line; the rope had knotted up and was taking extra time. She thought only for a second, and reached for the start button and started the engine. As it came to life, Jack got the stern line free and headed for the helm.

Jack and Melissa were almost in a dance during the hauling. Melissa had to remember that there was an extra five feet of boat, but she was quick enough; it didn't matter. Melissa noticed the camera man kept his distance this time. Jack whipped the boat around for the re-set and Melissa had to hold on tight. Jack's boat handled like a Ferrari; it was quick and nimble for a 38-footer.

"Stand back at the rail and hold on to the rope. It gets a little sketchy coming into the dock." Jack yelled back after the last trap went off the stern.

Like a slalom skier, *Red At Night* made the turns into the dock. The wake from the bounced off the dock splashed up on Melissa, but she remained focused and held tight onto the rope. She waited to hear the *Red At Night*'s diesel engine slow and shift into reverse. As soon as she felt the deck shift under her feet, she leaped up and tied the boat. She took off up the ramp. Corey and Ryan were looking at the stop watches and waving to her and Jack to go faster. She sprinted to the top, with Jack running behind her. As he crested the top of the ramp, Corey, Ryan, and the timers all jumped high. Melissa and Jack had not only won but had beat the record. Melissa jumped up onto Jack, wrapping her legs around him, and he wrapped his hands around her. They kissed while in each other's arms. There were some paparazzi there, trying to get pictures, but the locals either intentionally or accidentally would not allow them to get too close.

"Well, folks, we have a brief intermission while we move up to the Elementary School for the rest of the events. Please go grab some lunch at one of our local restaurants. Congratulations to all of our winners today." announced Corey.

"What are we going to do during the intermission, Jack?" asked Melissa.

"We have to go put the boat on the mooring, then grab some lunch at The Harbor."

"So, we have a little bit of…. time then, out on the mooring…." Melissa said playfully, giving Jack a kiss on the lips.

Jack grinned back and pointed to the boat.

***

Later in the afternoon, people started coming into the Elementary School. As Jack and Melissa walked into the school, the feeling of nostalgia washed over Jack. He remembered his mom and dad taking his picture in the "big hole," a big empty circle in the concrete just outside the doors going in. He remembered the fear and curiosity he felt. He remembered his father saying, "You will be alright; I will be right here when you get out, be good, kiddo." Now, in the not-so-distant future, he and Melissa would be doing very much the same thing. In the gymnasium, the bleachers were stretched out, and tarps were placed on the floor in front of 3 folding tables in front of the stage. They sat down with Russell, Anne, Lucy, and Sam. Russell went up to do the scallop shucking. One of his many childhood jobs was shucking scallops for seafood retailers. He had such a knack for it that he could carry on conversations while he was shucking, often not watching his hands. It added an element of entertainment. Anne did the shrimp picking competition. Jack told Melissa that his mother used to pick shrimp part-time when he and Lucy were kids. Russell and Anne came in second and first, respectively. They watched the net mending, and then came the lobster eating contest. Josh and Melissa went up and took spots behind the table. They were each given two lobsters, and lobster crackers (set of pliers for cracking lobster shells). Josh had gloves on his hands. Corey went on to explain the rules. The contestants would have to eat the body, knuckles, and claws of both lobsters. Once finished, the contestant was to put both hands in the air and yell, "done." Jack noticed that Abigail and Lizzy had taken positions behind Melissa.

"Here we go with the final event of the day." announced Ryan. "We would like to thank all of our sponsors and volunteers. This weekend couldn't happen without your help."

"Contestants, take your mark…." started Corey.

"Wait!" shouted Melissa. "I am not ready!"

As if on cue, Abigail and Lizzy pulled out and unfolded a padded folding chair, in which Melissa sat down. Lizzy tied a bib around Melissa's neck while Abigail poured a glass of what looked to be Chardonnay into a wine glass. Lizzy also took out a small container of melted butter and put it in front of Melissa.

"What is going on over here?" asked Ryan.

"If I am going to have Maine lobster, I will enjoy it. Not to mention, with the five-dollar entry fee, it's the best deal in town!" Melissa took a sip from the wine glass. It was actually just sparkling cider. "I am ready now!"

"Alright, on your mark, get set, Go!"

Melissa gently took apart her lobster, picking pieces out and letting them soak in butter. She then picked out some more and swapped it for the piece soaking in the butter. She dabbed at the corners of her mouth with a napkin. While taking another sip from the glass, she looked at the other end of the table. It was now clear why Josh was wearing gloves. He wasn't using the lobster crackers. He was smashing the knuckles and claws with his hands. And shoving the meat down his throat, then taking a gulp of water. Melissa turned back to her lobsters and gave a little wave to the crowd. She had just started cracking the claws on her first lobster when she heard Josh yell, "Done!"

"Time is one minute and fifty-one seconds!" Ryan announced. "Hold on, folks, we have to inspect the shells."

"Ryan, it looks to me that he may have eaten some of the shells too. I say the time stands. We have a new record!"

There was a bit of cheering while the other contestants finished up. Melissa finished last. The Boothbay Register managed to get a good picture of Melissa toasting the crowd. Josh sat down with Tylar Michaud, who beat him in the trap hauling contest, to talk about the upcoming lobster season and lobster boat racing season.

"Well, that was a fun day!" said Melissa after sitting down next to Jack. "I just love this town."

"I didn't expect Michael to do that. He has been hounding me to let me run with him for years." said Jack.

"I think after watching ole' Hollywood here, he figured if you guys were going to beat Ryan and Corey, she had to go with you. Next year, I think he intends to let Josh run *Overtime* next year and go with him. Now that will be a fast run."

Russell had reached out to Agent Rand and invited her down to watch Tall Tails and hang out with her "harbor family," as he called them. She was apprehensive at first, knowing she would have an FBI agent not far from her at all times. Agent Roberts volunteered for the duty and convinced Rand she should go and get some "human time." Tall Tails was just what she needed. Locals getting up on stage and telling funny stories and jokes. Melissa had taken the stage doing celebrity impersonations, Jack and Michael did a duo stand -up comedy skit. Agent Rand laughed like she hadn't laughed in a while. She needed it; she thought it was funny nobody brought up the events of last summer. Like an unwritten code had been placed that Tommy McIntire was to be forgotten.

"Russell, can I talk to you for a little bit?" Agent Rand asked Russell.

Russell could tell this was to be a private conversation. "Sure, let's step outside and get away from this noise." While walking outside, Russell noticed a large, red headed man keeping an eye on Carla. "Looks like we have company." Russell stated.

"That is what I want to talk to you about. Did you hear about Agent Ross?"

"No, I was in the hospital for a while. How is he?"

"Dead, he is dead, Russell. Balfour killed him, and now he is after me." Carla gave Russell a minute to comprehend what she had just told him. "While investigating his death, they discovered that Dan, Agent Ross, was actually working for Balfour." She continued on, telling him how now the FBI was watching her, thinking she was a part of it as well. She introduced Agent Andy Roberts and how he was one of the good guys. She told him of the suspected human trafficking and how she had been looking into disappearances in Maine. She had made some distant connections with an online used furniture store, but nothing concrete. She also mentioned the mysterious John Smith character who had asked Tommy about Melissa. When she was done telling him what was going on, his head sank, and when he talked, it was as if he was talking to the floor.

"What is this world coming to kid?" Russell asked Carla.

Carla Rand, who normally hated any kind of nickname, didn't mind being called kid by Russell, if anything, it felt like a warm blanket. She had a father, and he was a good man, but Russell just had that father to everyone feel to him.

"I don't know, Russell, it scares me, Balfour scares me; I didn't realize what I was getting into. First it was just Tommy dealing drugs, then murder, then the Russians, then Balfour. On top of that, I fell for Dan. I was waiting for him to show up to our first date while Balfour and his men were beating him to death. Then, to find out Dan was helping him. Balfour wanted revenge on the Russians for bypassing him in their drug dealing. Balfour is supposed to get a cut of everything that happens east of New York. If someone buys just an ounce of marijuana, Balfour gets a cut somewhere. If someone buys an illegal gun, Balfour gets a cut. The only thing keeping me safe is that the FBI is watching me like a hawk, but we suspect they have someone in the FBI again, but we are not sure."

"What can the Finn family do to help?"

"Just keep your eyes open and head on a swivel. I don't want to start a panic, so let's keep this between us for now."

"What about Lizzy? She was the whole reason you guys were able to take down that operation. You think they would go after her?"

"I don't know how much Dan told Balfour about her. Agent Roberts and I have been keeping tabs on Lizzy, and she has been in contact with us as well. Listen, Russell, I don't want to ruin your evening. I just wanted you to be aware of what is going on. You know this town, if something is out of place, you would know it."

"I will keep my eyes peeled. I know you will nail him eventually. Keep your chin up, kid. Hey, are you two staying down here tonight?"

The question caused Carla to pause a bit. Her and Andy had booked separate rooms down here so she wouldn't have to drive home. Russell could see the awkwardness of his question.

"Christ I ain't asking if you two are getting in a family way! I am trying to invite you to Finn Family breakfast tomorrow. Can ya' make it?"

"Yes, Mr. Finn. You had me at breakfast!" Agent Roberts answered.

"Great; I will tell Anne we got a couple extra coming! You will love it." Russell darted off to find Anne.

The scene in Anne's kitchen the next morning could only be described as a cornucopia of organized chaos. With Agent Roberts attending and given his southern roots, Anne added breakfast burritos and grits to the Finn Family breakfast menu. Along with

Carla and Andy, the Williams family, Clive Farrin, and Liam had come to join them. Anne fired the big grill outside, with Melissa making the sausage gravy and Abigail cooking bacon and sausage. In the kitchen, she had Carla making the stuffing for the burritos, which consisted of eggs, sausage, onion, jalapenos, mushroom, and green peppers. Lizzy was tasked with the blueberry pancakes and omelets, while Lucy was on biscuits, coffee, and juice detail. Anne couldn't remember ever having so many guests over. There was nothing she loved more than a full kitchen and sharing the knowledge with younger generations, even outside of her family. She circulated around, checking on everyone and helping when she could. Carla and Lucy had started asking Lizzy about Liam. She kept claiming he was just a friend. She was concerned about how Liam was doing, knowing the battery of questions he would be subjected to and how he would handle it with his stutter.

Russell had backed the 57 Chevy Belair out of the garage and into the driveway. All the guys were standing around looking at the car. Still shiny with no dirt on it at all. Russell had only backed it out of the garage a couple times to run it a bit. Russell could see that Andy Roberts felt a little awkward, not really knowing anyone here.

"Agent Roberts, Carla says you're from North Carolina, what do you do for fun down there?"

"You can call me Andy; I may have my gun and badge on me, but I am definitely off duty. I did a lot of motocross when I was younger; we have a few state and national parks. The coast looks like Maine, except not so rocky, and we catch shrimp, not lobster. Same kind of bars, restaurants, and stores. Just with different accents."

Andy could sense there were more questions on everyone's minds. Did they think there was something going on between him and Carla? Were they suspicious on why an FBI agent would be hanging around a DEA agent? Had Carla told them what was going on?

"What gun do you carry? If you don't mind me asking," Michael asked.

"I carry a Glock 22, you're Michael, right? I heard you are a pretty good shot. You and your daughter."

"Christ, Andy, don't get him talking about guns, you will never shut him up." jested Jack.

"When you going for the first cruise, Russell?" asked Sam as he slid his hand down the fender.

"Friday, after we are done at The Harbor, we will come home, change up, and head right back to The Harbor for dinnah, then go for a ride downtown." answered Russell

Liam stood just to the side of Josh, not hidden but trying not to be noticed.

"Liam, what's your plan for this summer?" asked Jack in an effort to get him in the conversation.

Liam's face started to warm. "I-I-I- p-p-plan on working a-a-a-at Knickerbocker c-c-c-amp."

Michael decided to speak before the silence became awkward. "Your interest, though, is in robots, right. You are looking at that tech school in Texas."

"Y-y-y-yes, I-I-I am on the s-s-s-school robot team." Liam said, with his face turning redder with every syllable.

"Liam, you have nothing to be nervous or embarrassed about. We don't judge in this family. You have obviously earned Michael's respect. Don't cut your words short because of that stutter. Say what you want to say." said Russell

"The new shop teacher speaks highly of you. Says you're a wiz of an engineer."

Liam relaxed a bit and became more involved in the conversion. The fact was, this group of men were not just protective of Lizzy, she respected them all and wanted them to respect him as well, even her little brother Josh. Josh was a character in himself. A freshman, but the size of a senior, bigger than more than half of the seniors. Despite that, he was in drama club in the lead role. Josh had told him not to tell his father, which confused Liam. Michael didn't seem to be the judging type. He was receptive to Liam and his stutter.

Andy took in the conversation and the general atmosphere. He didn't feel like an outsider, more of an observer. There was a feeling of something old-fashioned here among these people. They seemed more real than anyone he had ever met. These folks really cared about people. Carla had told them that they were the best people she knew, and she wasn't lying.

Lizzy came out and announced breakfast was ready. As Liam walked by Lizzy, he took her hand and then walked to the picnic table, holding hands. All observed this, but nobody mentioned it. Some moments shouldn't be interrupted.

Michael and Jack headed for the front of the line with their plates.

"You two chowdah heads know better than that. We have three guests here that ain't never been here before. They go first!" Said Anne.

Jack and Michael sheepishly stepped back from the table.

"Liam, Carla, and Andy, go ahead before those gulls eat everything!" jested Russell.

"I made your omelet myself," said Lizzy as she gave him a warm smile. She stood behind the table and had the omelets labeled for those who asked for one.

Anne and Russell always got their plates last. After filling their plates, they went to the table, each of them sitting on the ends. As he sat, he looked down the table, between the friends and family, and looked at his wife. She was as radiant as ever, glowing with the love and care she had for hosting these breakfasts. To Anne, these were much more than a meal. They were bonding, tradition, humility, and hospitality. She looked down at the table at him and smiled, and he did the same. Neither of them realized that the entire table was watching the moment. Nobody spoke a word.

Liam looked up from his plate to realize he was sitting across from Melissa. He was sitting directly across from a Hollywood actress, or she used to be one; she was still very famous. She was also one of Lizzy's closest friends. Melissa looked over at him and caught him staring. He felt panicked and nervous, but she smiled at him and spoke. "I know; I can hardly believe I am here either." Several at the table chuckled, while Lizzy gave him a nudge to the ribs.

"Lizzy, don't be so hard on him," said Anne. "Just look at this table. We have several lobstermen, a DEA agent, an FBI agent, a marine diesel mechanic, and a retired Hollywood actress, three high school students, and I don't know what to call Abigail and me. It's not every day you get to sit across from someone who has been in the movies, not just once but several times."

"I am afraid you don't ever really retire from being a celebrity. I still get calls from producers and directors; people still want autographs; just the other day there was this weird guy at The Harbor wearing a black hat, shady glasses, and a mask."

Both Carla and Andy stopped and looked at each other. Nobody caught their concerned look.

"Yeah, after he walked out, he stopped and looked back. I couldn't tell if he was looking over the harbor or trying to look back at Melissa. I asked him if he needed anything. He said he was a fan of us both and that I had a good girl, and to take care of her; kind of an odd thing for a fan to say."

"I don't want to talk about my life this whole breakfast. Lizzy, how is the prom planning coming along?" stated Melissa.

"So far, so good; the teachers were really happy I came up with six chaperones, even happier when I said we had two federal agents. We are doing it at the Botanical Gardens and having food catered in. It's going to look like a fancy outside ball." Lizzy answered.

"Sounds like it will be quite a night. Thanks for inviting me, Lizzy." said Agent Rand.

The conversation was drowned out by the sound of silverware against plates. Andy could not remember the last time he had such a big breakfast. It was like Thanksgiving; so much food and such variety, it was hard to stop.

"Anne and Russell, thank you for inviting me and Carla. The food was incredible, and you guys are such great people."

"Thank you, Andy; glad you liked it," answered Russell.

"How long have you been doing this?"

"Well, I don't remember exactly when we started, or why. I think we invited Clive and a couple others over, and it kind of stuck since then. It got to be really important when the kids got older. They were always so busy that we had to have just one meal; we sat down and talked as a family. As soon as everyone is done eating, we go through our highs and lows of the week and our goals for the next week. Although, with fourteen of us and we have the blessing of the fleet to get to, we may have to skip that and move forward to the next part."

"What is that?" Asked Andy

"You, and the rest of the men, have to clean my kitchen, and don't forget the grill." Anne said.

"In that case, I am going to get some more biscuits and gravy," jested Andy.

After everyone was done eating, the guys took to cleaning up the kitchen, while the women sat outside and talked. Carla was soaking up all this…people time. She had been so secluded since Dan died and being under suspension. This was just what she needed to breathe in some new energy, energy she would need to take down Balfour.

The guys finished cleaning, and they all headed down to The Harbor to get into boats for the blessing of the fleet. Liam, Lizzy, and Josh went in Josh's boat, while Michael and Abigail went in Michael's. Andy, Carla, Lucy, and Sam went with Jack and Melissa in Jack's boat. Russell and Anne had *Old Smoke* to themselves. They could hear the preacher announcing the names of people lost at sea over the radio. A solemn reminder of just how risky working on the water was. Then, just as they had for Zeke's boat parade, all the local fishermen then lined up. This time, smallest to largest boats , with the Coast Guard last.

"Jack, let me run the boat, and you can give Carla and Andy a little history of the area and the blessing of the fleet."

Jack stepped away from the helm and started pointing out the different historical points of Boothbay Harbor. He glanced at Melissa every once and a while, but she seemed confident at the helm.

"The blessing of the fleet is a European tradition that is centuries old. The priest blesses each boat, wishing it a safe and bountiful season." Jack announced, as the first boat, which was Josh, went by the priest at the dock.

No different than Zeke's boat parade, as soon as Josh was clear of the dock and other traffic, he hit the throttle and sent *Tip Jar* skimming about the water like a stone. Other boats in line followed suit. Melissa didn't hesitate when it was *Red At Night*'s turn. She told Jarvis, who was standing up on the bow, to lay down. Slowly creeping the throttle up, she kept one hand on the wheel. She had to get up on her tip toes until the boat planed off. Jack's boat handled much differently than Russell's. It seemed to skate on top of the water, and the steering was quicker. They passed Russell and Anne in the *Old Smoke*; she could see Michael and Abigail ahead of her in the *Overtime*. Michael let her get beside him, and the two boats raced. When Melissa had run out of throttle, Michael slowly added more and slid past them. After the wake died down, they tied up alongside each other to talk and relax.

"Jack, is there any fish around here?" asked Andy.

"No, still too early. You come back in June and I will take you to get some stripers," answered Jack.

"I will be sure to do that!"

After hanging out on the water and enjoying the day and the company, they headed back into the dock, and everyone headed home. Jack, Melissa, and Jarvis came through the door and sat down on the couch, Jarvis with his head on Melissa's lap, while she leaned into Jack, who had his arm up on her shoulders.

"Annnnnd that is your first Fisherman's Festival Weekend! What was your favorite part?" asked Jack.

"The intermission yesterday," replied Melissa with a devilish grin.

"How can you say that after a priest just threw holy water at us this morning?" Jack said, jokingly.

"Oh, is that what that was…. I thought I felt something burning."

"What am I going to do with you?"

"I don't know, but I am going up to bed and taking off my clothes to find out."

She stood up, took her hooded sweatshirt off, tossed it on the floor, and started taking off her t-shirt while walking up the stairs.

"Jarvis… Stay!" said Jack as he followed Melissa up the stairs, catching her bra on the way.

Chapter 11

"I don't understand why we are going to this musical. Lizzy and Liam have gone out on dates before without us." Michael said, while straightening his tie.

"Because I want to go and watch. You are my husband, and you are taking me." Abigail said while putting in earrings.

"Why do I have to get all dressed up? It's a High School musical, not Broadway."

"Because you are taking your wife on a date! If you continue to whine and complain, you will be sleeping on the couch or out in your shop."

"Yes, mam."

Michael and Abigail walked down the stairs to see Lizzy and Liam in the kitchen, waiting for them. Michael sensed there was more going on here than he knew.

"Where is Josh? How is he getting out of this?"

"Josh is going to meet us there; he is going with a friend."

They all got into Michael's truck and headed for the High School. While looking for a parking spot, he saw Melissa's Blazer, but he knew she was helping the drama club. Then he saw Anne's car. "Probably supporting Melissa," he thought to himself. He parked the truck and they all went in. Michael tried to pay the cover for all of them, but Liam insisted on paying for Lizzy. Since Abigail and Lizzy grabbed programs, he decided not to. Abigail guided them to some seats that were in the front row. "Reserved for Family of Josh Williams" they said.

"O.K.…. What gives?" Michael asked.

Without a word, Abigail folded the front of the program back and passed it to Michael, pointing to the top of the page. Michael read the first name.

Josh Williams as Marty McFly

"What! Josh in a musical?" Michael stammered.

"The lead role in a musical, and Melissa says he is very good."

Before Michael could say anything, the lights went dim, and the play started.

Josh came out onto the stage, and Michael was in awe of how confident he was and how natural it came to him. The next scene was the first musical number, and Michael watched and listened to his son sing. During the whole play, Michael was fixed on watching his son. Josh was a natural. He had the audience captivated. At the end of the play, Josh walked out onto the stage to bow to the audience, and Michael roared above the crowd.

"That's my boy! That is my son!"

The performers eventually came out from backstage to greet their families. Josh still had his costume on when he walked up to his family. After receiving hugs from his mother and sister, he turned to face his father. He was tall enough to see eye to eye with his father now. Michael stood looking at his son, knowing why this had been kept secret. He never spoke highly of people in the entertainment industry. "Melissa is alright, but the rest of them think they are better than everyone," was his common phrase among several others that were much worse. If he hadn't been so proud, he would have been consumed with the guilt of making his son feel he couldn't talk to him. His son had taught him a lesson, and he was grateful. Michael stuck out his hand to shake Josh's and then pulled him to a hug.

"I am proud of you." he said.

"Thanks Dad." Josh replied.

Russell, Anne, and Jack came over to congratulate Josh, followed by Lucy and Sam. They could see Melissa talking to a woman from the audience. Then she brought her to the group.

"Hello everyone, this is Renee Finlay from Dirigo Talent Agency; Renee, this is Josh and his family," Melissa introduced the lady to the group.

"Hello Josh, great job tonight; we have a musical coming up at the State Theatre in Portland, and I want you in it. You will still have to audition, but for you, that's just a formality. You basically have the part if you want it. It is a paid role." Renee said, passing him a card.

"Ah, yeah, OK, I will be in touch." Josh replied.

Later on that evening, Josh was in his room watching motorcross fail videos when he heard a knock on the door.

"Come in."

Michael walked in and leaned on the door frame. "Hey, I want to talk to you a bit."

Josh paused the video, and Michael took the chair from the desk and sat down. "Look, I don't want to talk about why you kept that a secret from me; I get it. I do want to make a few things clear. I will always love you, no matter what you do in life. I never meant to push you in any direction by having you turn wrenches with me. I always thought it was our thing. Like how Lizzy and I have shooting. If you do this, this acting and singing, you give it your all. No half-assin' it. You hear?"

"Dad I can still turn wrenches with you and be an actor. I like working on stuff with you. I never once thought you would love me less or not be proud of me. I just wanted to surprise you."

"Well, you certainly surprised me. I mean, I've heard you sing in the shop, and it sounded good. Tonight was incredible. You have something, Josh."

Josh held up his fist, and Michael returned in kind with a fist bump and left the room.

Demitri Balfour toured his new yacht that had been delivered. He had his men convert a couple of the state rooms to holding cells. Insulating the compartments against sound, making sure anything that could be used to escape was removed, and upgrading the locks. His customers for the auction had all been vetted. It had turned out that both Agent Rand and Melissa Andrews would be at the same place at the same time, according to his new contact in the FBI. He knew just the way to grab them and get them to his yacht. They were going to be chaperoning the High School prom together. His new contact would cause an issue to draw them to the ladies' bathroom together. They would be injected with a sedative, then loaded into a van, where they would be bound and hooded. From that point, Paul would kill the FBI contact, then take the ladies to a dock in Boothbay Harbor, where a boat would be waiting. From there, a short run to where his new yacht would be waiting on the west side of Squirrel Island. Once onboard and put into the converted staterooms, he would bring them up individually for auction. Once the auction was over, it was up to the winning parties to get their merchandise off the yacht. He would allow use of the boat, and the yacht had a helicopter pad. There were several small airfields and docks they could use. Once all the participants had gone, he and Paul would set the course for the yacht's autopilot to head into the harbor and crash into the Finn's restaurant. He would shoot Paul before getting into a small tender. He would disappear, never to be seen in the States again.

As April turned to May, deadlines seemed to be looming over Melissa's head. She had tracked down the dress that Michael had asked about for Lizzy. She knew he couldn't afford it and knew he wouldn't willfully let Melissa help. So, the price she told him was but a small fraction of the actual cost. Jack had warned her that if he ever found out, he would be mad. She had also had a seamstress that worked with her in the past, the very one that made the dress, pose as an employee at the dress shop where Abigail and Lizzy went dress shopping.

Prom was this Saturday; though Melissa had a lot of fun getting ready for prom, Melissa was anxious to get back to planning her wedding. Though it seemed to be much easier than the prom. Jack had already built a platform that would be set in *Red At Night*. It had a waist high railing and was trimmed with driftwood that Jack and the other lobstermen had collected. Anne and Lucy were taking care of the reception details. This Sunday, at family breakfast,she and Jack were going to announce that she was pregnant. Even though Russell, Anne, Lucy, and Sam knew already, she couldn't wait to announce it and make it official. They hadn't decided if they were going to announce the names yet or wait. She took a sip of her decaf tea. Even though her doctor had said small amounts of coffee were fine, Melissa had refrained from all caffeine and alcohol. Today, she would be volunteering at the high school by helping the music teacher. After finishing her tea, she got herself ready and headed out the door.

Jack was loading his boat with traps at the Finn family dock. Michael was there, helping load traps.

"Less than a month away, my friend, and you will be a married man. You two going to start having kids right away or wait a bit?" asked Michael

"I think we will wait. I mean, we just got a dog a couple months ago, and we just started living together," Jack answered, suppressing a grin.

"How is that going?"

"Well, you remember how that goes. I won't get into the details, but we don't sleep much. You can tell she is used to having someone pick up after her. She sometimes leaves glasses or mugs out. She doesn't mean to, and if I don't pick them up, she will in the morning. That's her routine; she has a quick cleaning fit every morning, running around the house picking things up before she leaves. She took my coffee the other day, and I wasn't even done with it."

"Has she gotten after you yet for anything?"

"Typical stuff; toilet seat, TP roll sitting on the counter rather than on the holder. Parking my truck diagonally in the driveway, she really hates that but doesn't say anything about it. She knows I leave the keys in it, so she just jumps in and moves it."

"Sounds like you two are doing just fine."

"Yeah, almost too good. I get nervous, like something is going to go wrong at any minute. I mean, we haven't been together that long. It seems like we have been at wide open throttle since I picked her out of the water."

"Jack, I don't know what to tell you about that. You guys have something rare, in the truest sense of the word. Not only have you guys developed a solid relationship, and, in less than a year, you've been through more tests in than most couples in that time. You were damaged goods when you two first met. I think she was too, a little. You guys had to work from a negative balance. I think you guys are going to live long and happy lives together."

"Thanks, man."

⚜

Carla Rand looked out of her living room window. She could see the FBI agents watching her house. The FBI had cut back on the surveillance. There were a pair of obvious agents in a Chevy Tahoe. You could see the government plates and the outlines of emergency lights in the grill. The unmarked agents that had been roaming around had been removed from the detail. Even though she was allowed to come and go as she pleased, it still agitated her that the FBI was always right there. Always following her, always listening. The time they were wasting following her, they could be used to get Balfour. Agent Andy Roberts often visited her, keeping up the interrogations about Dan for those listening in. He was clever, always asking questions that had clues or hints about the case, so she would be able to figure out how the investigation into Balfour was going. He also would leave little notes that would help inform her of what was going on. The case was at a standstill. They had found a warehouse in Portland that had been abandoned. Some squatters were caught coming and going, and during the arrest, some blood was spotted on the floor. Forensics matched the blood to Dan's. The entire building was combed and combed again. Every square inch was processed. They had found a belt sander with human DNA in the grit. That DNA came back to the two thugs driving the box truck and one other unknown. That made sense because the two men in the truck had their fingerprints removed, because of the shotgun used. No facial or dental records could be matched. They both had ties with Demetri Balfour, but not enough for a warrant.

She couldn't wait for Lizzy's prom. It was another opportunity to get out of the house, even if she had to wear a dress. She had chosen a long dress so she could still carry her ankle holster, and a jacket so she could wear the knife Michael had given her. Only Andy would be following her that night. Though she trusted Andy, she wanted to have protection for herself just in case. That was the bad part of the FBI backing off on the surveillance, fewer people protecting her.

Russell was out on the dock, moving some empty crates around, when Sam walked down the ramp and onto the dock.

"Hey Russell, are you supposed to be doing that?" Sam asked.

"Yeah, this is ok. I have to get help with the full ones, but I am at the age I should get help with those anyway. I just have to be sure not to get winded. Since not smoking my pipe is getting harder and harder to get winded."

Sam had played this conversation in his head more than one hundred times over the past few weeks. Make some small talk, then ask for Russell's permission to marry Lucy. It seemed easy enough, and there was no logical reason to be worried. He had been dating Lucy for years now and they had been living together for months. Now, he had thought too long. Russell turned to him and looked as if he was waiting for him to say something.

Russell knew just what was going on inside Sam's head. While in a coma, Sam had talked about asking him for permission to marry Lucy. Now if the guy could just get the words out. He could make it easy for him, and say what he thought before Sam asked, but this was something Sam had to earn. It was an odd thing to be nervous about. He loved Sam and respected him. He knew Sam had felt like an outsider a little around him and Jack, even Michael. He and Jack were rough and tumble lobstermen, and Michael was a hardened Navy veteran and marine diesel mechanic. Sam had started bagging groceries at Hannaford's at 16 and climbed the ladder to manager when he had given it up to work at The Harbor. Russell respected that more than anything, giving up a job you had worked and excelled at to work for family you were not officially part of yet. Sam worked long hours at The Harbor, learned the lobster side of the business, and his knowledge of food and the grocery world was an asset for the restaurant side. Maybe it was about time he heard that.

"Sam, I have been meaning to talk to you. Pull up a crate and sit down."

Russell pulled up a crate and took a seat, while Sam did the same.

"Sam, I had a lot of time to think when I was on that bed. There is something I should have told you a while ago. Thank you! We were so busy getting this place off the ground that I forgot to thank one of the most crucial people. You not only knew the best deals where to get food and other supplies, you also knew the best place to get parts for the refrigerators and freezers. I will go even as far as saying that Jack and Melissa took a lot of attention away from you and Lucy. Sam, I am damn glad you are with us and stood by my daughter while I was in the hospital." Russell finished, putting the empty pipe back into his mouth. "There you go, kid,…I set it up; go for it," he thought in his head.

"Russell, I love Lucy with all my heart, with all that I am and all that I will be. She makes me a better person, and I think I do the same for her. That is enough right there for what I am going to ask you, but I also love you, Anne, Jack, and Melissa. I can't ask to join the family because I already know I am a part of it. I will ask for your daughter's hand in marriage?"

"Nothing would make me prouder or happier, Sam."

"Thank you, sir."

"Never mind that sir business; when are you going to ask her?"

"Saturday, at the prom. After the kids leave and we start picking up, I will ask the DJ to play our favorite song, then walk her on to the dance floor."

"Sam, that is wonderful."

The week went by fast as everyone was anticipating the prom. Michael and Lizzy had planned how to get Jack and Melissa out onto the dance floor after the kids had left. Michael would show up to take pictures of the dance and to talk with the DJ, if needed. Sam spent any moment he was alone practicing his proposal to Lucy. All the tuxes and dresses were fit and ready to go.

Friday night, Demetri Balfour called Paul and Andy into his office to discuss the plan.

"Paul, you will take the van to the Maine Botanical Gardens and park at the Bosarge Education Center. There is a restroom right there. You will have both the syringes with you, along with the bags and zip ties. Andy, Agent Rand is still under the impression that you are on her side, yes?"

"Yes, Mr. Balfour, she believes that I'm on her side and a dedicated FBI agent with a mission of putting you behind bars."

"Very good. I think it would be best that Paul handles things after the women are put into the van. I will want you to stay behind and tell us what the FBI is doing once they realize Agent Rand is missing. I will want you to make them believe she has taken Ms. Andrews."

"Sounds good, sir."

"Now you can go and keep an eye on Agent Rand. We are approaching the end of this, and I want no mistakes."

Andy Roberts left the office. Balfour waited to make sure he heard Andy's footsteps walking away.

"Paul, as soon as you have the women in the van, I want you to shoot that man dead. Use a suppressor. After that, I want you to transport the women to the dock, load them onto the boat, then bring them to the yacht."

Paul nodded in agreement.

Lizzy woke up early on Saturday morning. She had been so busy planning everything, she hadn't had time to think about prom. Prom was the beginning of the end. Soon there would be graduation, then one last summer, then packing up and leaving. The thought of leaving home thrilled her and horrified her at the same time. She would be headed to Texas. First, it would be the trip down. She had decided that she would make the drive herself, the first move in independence. Her thoughts were interrupted by a knock on the door.

"Come in," she said, knowing it was her mother by the gentle knock.

Abigail opened the door, while carrying a long white box with a velvet green bow.

"What is that, Mom?"

"Your prom dress, sweetie."

"My dress is hanging in the closet, mom. It's already been fit."

"Well, your father said you might like this one better."

Lizzy rolled her eyes. "Why? Does it come with an alarm and a GPS tracker? I know that is why he got the limo, so Josh can be his little watchdog. I wish he would trust me and Liam."

"Lizzy, it's a father thing, and before you say anymore, you may just want to open this." Abigail set the box down on Lizzy's bed. Lizzy untied the bow and removed the lid from the box. There it was; the emerald, green velvet dress she had seen Melissa wear in her movie, Over the Rainbow. It was a replica of the one Judy Garland had worn in her movie Easter Parade. She stared at the dress, running her fingers along the velvet. The lump in her throat would not permit her to speak. She looked up at her mother with her eyes glistening.

"He is out in the shop, working on the boat."

Lizzy sprang out of bed in her flannel pajamas and dashed down the stairs and across the lawn in her bare feet. Her father stood there with a cup of coffee in his hand. She gave him a big hug.

"Thank you, Daddy."

"No problem, kiddo. Have fun and be safe tonight."

Michael gave his daughter another hug and watched her go back to the house. He then texted Melissa, "Nailed it," to which she responded with a smiley emoji.

"Operation Green Dress a success; Operation Hollywood Prom to commence." He grabbed his phone and called Jack.

"Yeoo," answered Jack on the other end.

"Hey, Lizzy and I have been conspiring on a plan that involves you and your fiancé."

"Uhhh, ok… What is going on?"

"When she went shooting with us, she told me she never got a chance to have a prom. So, Lizzy and I put plan 'Hollywood Prom' into action. That is part of the reason she chose you two for chaperones. Your mother has been in on it too. She got your old letterman jacket from her attic and had it dry cleaned. I have it here, and I am going to bring it to you tonight. Once all the kids leave, you ask her to your prom and to have a dance. Then you put the coat on her. She will finally have her prom."

"Holy shit, Mike."

"What! What is wrong?"

"Nothing, I just figured out something I have been trying to figure out for years."

"What is that?"

"How a grumpy peckerhead like you ever got a woman like Abigail."

"I am not all piss and vinegar, Jack. I can also be the gangster of love; I am like Cupid and John McClane all rolled into one."

"Wow… weeeeellll any way, thank you,man."

"No problem, brothah. See ya latah!"

Agent Andy Roberts pulled up to Agent Rand's house. He still didn't dare trust any of the other members of the team. If Balfour had gotten to him, there was a strong possibility he may have gotten to someone else too. He took out a small notepad and wrote it down.

You and Melissa tonight. I am supposed to get both of you to go to the restroom, then they will snatch you. I think we act as soon as all of us are at the restroom. I will still be wearing a wire, so we can't talk about it at the prom.

He folded the piece of paper up and went to the door. After exchanging greetings, Agent Roberts started interrogating her as usual. He stuck the note under his coffee cup for her to see after he left. When he was done with his mock interrogation and briefing her about how he would follow her to the prom, he left the house. He thought about texting her what the note said on her spare phone, but if the FBI ever found it, he would be in trouble. Agent Rand decided to pick up her kitchen before getting ready. When she picked up the coffee cup, the note fell on the floor, under the kitchen table. The floor was looking a little dirty, so she started her rumba vacuum cleaner while she was in the shower. The rumba bounced its way around the room, eventually sucking up the note left by Andy Roberts.

The Williams house was a swarm of activity while Abigail and Anne helped get Lizzy and Hazel ready. Michael was getting Josh ready. Liam was waiting downstairs with Hazel's date. It was a bright and sunny day out so as soon as Josh's date had arrived, Abigail started taking pictures. After taking pictures, they all climbed into the limo and headed to the Maine Botanical Gardens for their prom.

At the Maine Botanical Gardens, the chaperones were helping get the final decorations up. Agent Andy Roberts kept looking for a sign from Carla that she had read the note, but she was so into this moment and having such a good time with Lucy and Melissa. He kept doubting his decisions. Should he contact his superior and let him know what was going on? He just didn't know how high up Balfour's reach was. It had been a month ago when Paul, Balfour's right-hand man, had approached him. The man had walked right up to him and said, "Come with me." Andy stared at him blankly, about to challenge him and ask just who he thought he was. Then Paul passed him a manilla envelope, almost as if he were in a spy movie. Andy slid the contents of the envelope out. He was looking at a picture of himself; himself and a blonde teenager getting into his car. Then more of him with the teenager getting out of his car and going into his apartment with him. More and more pictures of them eating together in Boothbay Harbor. "Come with me." He got into Paul's Mercedes, and he drove to Commercial Street, then to the very edge of Portland Yacht Services, where the older delinquent boats were left. Paul pulled in, and a tall man came walking out from between two boats.

"Agent Roberts, how wise of you to cooperate with us." Said Demetri Balfour.

"I never said I was going to cooperate." Andy Roberts responded coolly.

"Well, it would be in your best interest if you did. Those pictures, along with the pictures of you riding with Paul and meeting with me here, will find themselves into the hands of the FBI."

"Those pictures with the girl show nothing. She could be a sister or a cousin. All of this could be explained."

"Yes... yes, it could," Balfour sighed a bit, almost as if empathetic. "But...you have no sisters or cousins of that age. It would be very hard to explain this visit since I just deposited $100,000 into your bank account. I also have someone at the FBI that would push those photos in front of the right eyes. Now, you can work for me, keep that money, and make lots more, or I turn those photos in, and the career you have built dwindles away to nothing, then I kill you, like I killed Dan Ross."

Andy Roberts stood there with a blank expression. This moment was tough; if he showed too much emotion, it would give him away. Carla, Commissioner Stryker, and him had worked this out. Using Lizzy not as bait but for ammunition for blackmail. They knew Carla was being watched, so Roberts stayed in the view as much as possible and turned himself into a target.

Now with the plan getting close to its apex, he started thinking of the things that could go wrong. He had just learned the following night about abducting not only Carla but Melissa Andrews as well. If Carla had read the note, everything would be all set.

The dance area looked magical. Daffodils, tulips, lilies, and even some early lupines surrounded the pavilion. Soft amber lights were strung up along the tree branches, and the smell of lilacs filled the air. A fire was glowing in the outdoor fireplace, making itself known by small pops and crackles. Tall ivory white tables and chairs surrounded the dance floor. A buffet table with a collection of finger foods and drinks was set off to the side. Mellisa walked to the middle of the dance floor and slowly spun around to take it in. She could hear the kids coming up the walkway, guided by the soft glow of candles, in white paper bags. She wanted just a few more seconds to take in the moment, but she wanted the floor to be clear. As if the other chaperones heard her thoughts, they all took positions outside of the area. As soon as the kids started to walk in, the DJ started with music. Melissa moved to a point where she could see kids walking up the hill to come in.

She saw Lizzy walking and holding hands with Liam; Melissa was taken aback at just how stunning she was in the green dress with her hair and makeup all done. The black tux Liam wore helped the dress pop even more. What looked the best to Melissa, though, was Lizzy's smile. The seventeen year old girl, who looked to be in her twenties right now, had a childish, angelic smile that gave hints of her youth and innocence. She looked at all the kids coming in, almost with an air of envy that she never got to experience any of this. Not just prom, but adolescence, coming of age, growing up, and growing forward. She was suddenly startled by a set of hands on her hips, then calmed by the gentle kiss on the top of her head.

"What are you thinking?" Jack said, softly.

"I am happy our child is going to grow up without spotlights and microphones. He or she will grow up as normal as possible. We will slowly change from active participants to proud spectators. We will watch them grow, Jack; watch them grow, learn, get hurt, get back up, and grow more. We will do this together, Jack. Together and with your family, we will have two great kids just like Lizzy and Josh, maybe even more."

Jack had no idea what to say; there was nothing to say. Another kiss on the top of the head was enough to say he agreed. He let the moment rest, like savoring the flavor of a favorite candy. Then, with his hands, he gently turned her towards him and rested his forehead on hers.

"For crying out loud you two! We are supposed to be the adults here! Stop the hanky panky and start keeping an eye on the kids!" Lucy barked.

"Okay, okay sis, thanks for ruining our moment."

"You two ain't supposed to be having a moment. You are supposed to be keeping an eye on these kids and making sure they aren't spiking the punch or running off to have some hanky panky themselves."

"How about you and I take a walk over to the punch bowl and check it out then," Jack fired back jokingly.

"I will go find Sam and take a walk around and see if we can find any hanky pankiers," Melissa continued the jesting.

"You two are made for each other; you know that, right!"

Melissa found Sam and asked him to walk with her. Sam was the one member of the Finn family she never really got a chance to talk to.

"How are you and Lucy doing?" Melissa asked.

"We are doing really good. Actually, between you and me, after the last dance and the kids are all gone, I am going to walk Lucy on to the dance floor and ask her to marry me! I am so nervous, I left my phone down in the car, but I have the ring!"

"Oh my, that is great! The Finn family keeps getting bigger and bigger. It just occurred to me that you and I are kind of in the same boat. Marrying into the family, I mean."

"Yeah, but you don't ever feel outside of the family, do you? I remember picking up Lucy for her first date. Pulling right into the Finn family compound. All of them were outside. Russell and Jack were both smiling, but when I shook their hands, they had grips like a vise; not intimidating, but you knew they were there. Anne had that same piercing look she had with you on the boat. I felt a bit out of place at first, being a grocery clerk among the rough and tough fishing family, but they started asking questions about work and what I did. For a moment, I thought about asking to just stay there for our date and talk to the family. It wasn't but a couple days later, I had a flat tire on the way to work. Jack pulled up and started to help. I said I was fine, but he stayed there anyway, keeping his headlights on and flashers going to help keep me safe. My spare was in horrible shape. Jack took me to work, took care of my tire and the spare. Then he dropped my car off at work. Obviously, I paid him for the tire and the spare, but he never asked for it. I asked him a few weeks later why. He said he had never seen his sister so happy. I guess she was beaming after the first date. It was something I said."

"What did you say?"

"Well, she made a comment about her...size. How she is a large-framed woman. I told her I didn't care; she was kind, funny, and made me laugh. That was all I needed, and that I had been wanting to ask her out for a while."

"Sam, that's just awesome. I am going to be proud to call you my brother-in-law."

"Let us leave out the 'in-law' part, and you just be a sister, ok?"

The moment was interrupted by Agent Roberts.

"Melissa, there is a girl that needs help in the bathroom. Can you go with Carla and help her out?"

"Sure, later Sam."

Agent Roberts walked away; he took out his phone and called Paul.

"They are headed your way now. I will be right behind them. Have the van ready to roll."

He sure hoped Carla had read his note. He knew she had a gun on her; she would have it out and ready to go before she got to the bathroom. But…as he walked a distance behind her, he noticed she wasn't getting ready. She hadn't read the note. She and Melissa were walking into an ambush. He started to pick up his pace.

Twenty yards behind Agent Roberts was Sam. Sam had overheard the phone call, and it didn't sound good. When Agent Roberts picked up his pace, Sam's concerns grew more.

Back at the dance area, Lucy and Jack were standing and watching the kids on the dance floor. The music was a selection of old rock and roll with newer music as well. Even a few classic hits from Elvis and Aretha Franklin. Jack found himself proud of Lizzy when she knew all the words to Def Leppard's "Pour Some Sugar on Me."

"Jack, do you remember being that young? How simple life was, but yet we thought it was so tough."

"Oh yeah, now look at us. You and Sam have been living together for a while, Melissa and I are getting married and having a baby."

"You and Melissa are not the only ones getting married…"

"Are you serious? Did Sam propose?"

"Not yet, but the goober left the receipt in his pants pocket. That and Dad has been acting funny."

"Ha ha ha, I think dad is the better indicator than the receipt."

"Oh ya, he has that Russell Finn glow going on. Asking about me and Sam, how are we doing. You know."

"Well, I am happy for you Lucy."

Bang!

Bang!

Bang!

"Jack, what was that?"

"I don't know. It sounded like gun shots, but it could have been some kid shooting off fireworks or something. You stay up here. I will check it out."

Jack started walking quickly towards the sound, in the direction of the restrooms.

154

Chapter 12

Melissa and Carla walked to the restroom together, chatting about the evening and what could possibly be going on in the restroom. Neither of them noticed Agent Roberts trying to close the gap between them, nor did they notice Sam further behind him. Agent Rand saw a dark blue van and was curious about what it was doing there. The DJ and caterers were all parked up by the café, and it was much too late for any staff to be there. She slowed down her pace a bit and started surveying the area. Melissa had rounded the van before she could tell her to stop. He heard Melissa make an odd noise and didn't hear her footsteps anymore. Agent Rand stopped in her tracks. When she did, a large man stepped from around the van. He looked at her only momentarily, then passed her.

"Grab her quickly!" yelled the man.

She didn't dare to turn around to see who he was taking to. She dropped to one knee, putting her left leg in front so she could grab the Glock 43 out of the ankle holster, but it was one moment too long. The man had pulled a suppressed pistol out of the inside of his coat. She put her hands up while still holding her Glock.

"Drop the weapon." he said as he tossed what looked like a syringe to someone behind her. She didn't dare turn to see. She put the Glock down while looking at his suppressed firearm. She heard the footsteps come closer. Then, she heard a very familiar voice whisper, "Play dead." Then she felt a wet feeling, like some fluid was just squirted inside of the neck of her jacket, but not injected like she anticipated. She closed her eyes and fell limp on the ground. She heard that same familiar voice, the voice of agent Andy Roberts say to the other man, "Give me a bag and zip ties." He then zip tied her hands in front of her, then her ankles, put a hood over her head, and lifted her into the back of the van. Then, she felt them load Melissa into the van and close the van doors. She was waiting for Andy to make his move and arrest this guy.

Sam had watched it all happen and went for his cell phone until he realized he had left it in his car. He was trying to get the plate number of the van, but Agent Roberts was in the way. He saw Agent Rand's gun sitting on the ground, but there was no way he could get to it in time. The other man reached into his inside coat pocket again, pulled out the suppressed handgun again, and shot Agent Roberts three times in the chest. He went for a head shot, but the homemade suppressor had jammed the gun. He started to unscrew the suppressor. "Now is the time." Sam thought. He ran as fast as he could to Agent Rand's Glock 43 on the ground. Paul saw the man coming and started unscrewing the silencer faster. Sam dove for the gun and pointed it as best he could at Paul. Paul had dropped the suppressor and was bringing his gun around when Sam fired.

Bang!

Paul heard the bullet go past his left ear. He lined his sights up on the man on the ground's head and slowly squeezed the trigger.

Bang!

Before his gun went off, he heard another gunshot and felt an impact on his left shoulder. Then felt the report of his own gun going off.

Bang!

The man's head fell to the ground. He had been hit as well, but not lethal. With the three loud gun shots, the music that was coming from the dance had stopped. He got into the van and drove off as quickly as he could. As he was pulling away, he passed Jack Finn's truck going the other way. He thought about turning around and shooting Jack, but he needed to get out of there. It was a ten-minute ride to where the boat was, and nobody had a clue where he was headed. Boothbay Harbor only had two policemen on duty. The odds were in his favor. He could feel his arm getting wet with blood. He was hit, but if he could get to the boat, he would make it.

Jack could see two figures lying on the ground, so he broke into a sprint. He also saw a blue van leaving. He rolled the first body onto its back.

"Sam! What happened?"

Sam couldn't speak, and there was blood all over him. He just laid there, looking up at Jack, lazily opening and closing his eyes.

Jack heard a scream not too far in the distance. It was Lucy; she had come to check out the noise after checking on the kids. She ran to Sam, falling to her knees.

"Sam, hold on, Sam," she said, sobbing, while holding his hand.

Sam knew his time left with Lucy could be measured in seconds. He reached into his coat pocket and pulled out a black velvet box. With all the strength he had left, he reached up with it to hold it to Lucy. Everything was fading now and felt cold. Lucy took the velvet case and opened it. She burst into tears and said, "Yes."

As all sight and sound faded from Sam's senses, the last thing he heard was Lucy saying yes.

Jack heard a groan from the other man.

"He has them. Carla and Melissa. They are in the van. Don't call 911; they are listening to the police band. Call Commissioner Strykcr, take my phone, use the tracker app; Carla has a tracker on," said Agent Roberts in a series of grunts and gasps. The bullet proof vest had stopped the rounds, but the impact had cracked, possibly broken, his sternum and a few of the upper ribs.

Just then, Michael was pulling in with his truck.

"What the fuck is happening? Are the kids safe?"

"Yes, the kids are safe. You take this phone and watch the screen. Did you see a blue van?"

"Yeah, damn near ran…."

"Shut up and get into your truck, Michael; I am driving."

Jack jumped into the truck to find Jarvis sitting in the back seat; there was no time to ask why. He spun the truck around in a J-turn and pushed the pedal to the floor. The 7.3 powerstroke diesel roared while the back wheels spun a bit, then found traction. Michael held Roberts's cell phone while watching the tracking app while calling Commissioner Stryker and put him on speaker. Jack filled them both in on what had happened so far and where the van was heading. The Commissioner informed them that a man in black clothing had been seen snooping around Melissa's, and the Boothbay Harbor Police Department was busy looking for him.

⁂

Agent Rand had heard the gunshots and could only guess what happened. Andy must have tried to shoot Paul but missed, then Paul finished him off. Paul had a gun, which made him dangerous. She had to plan her moves accordingly. She wiggled her head to get the cloth bag off of her face so she could see. Both she and Melissa were side by side, with their heads towards the front of the van. She was directly behind the driver, so he couldn't see her. With a flick of her wrist, the extendable blade that Michael had given her came out. She twisted her arms around, so the blade cut the zip tie. Then she slowly pulled her legs up and cut the zip tie holding her ankles. She thought about trying to stab him and take control of the situation, but he was driving, and it could easily get them all killed. Melissa looked to be out cold but was still breathing. Now it was just a waiting game until he opened the door.

⁂

In Michael's truck, they continued tracking the van with the app on Agent Roberts' phone.

"He is on Barter's Island Road heading towards Lakeside Drive," Michael said.

"Michael, do you have a gun on you?"

"Yeah, but let's hope it doesn't come to that. He just made the right onto Lakeside Drive. My gut tells me he isn't going to Southport, the bridge, and it's basically a dead end. If he were going out of town, he would have headed towards the rotary. He is headed to town. I think he has a boat somewhere." Michael paused and watched the screen. Sure enough, it showed the icon taking

Middle Road and not staying on Lake Side Drive. "Yeah, just like I thought, he is taking the middle road. That works for us. For someone not from around here, that is a hard road to drive fast on. Especially in a damn van. You need to focus and drive like you never have before."

Jack didn't say a word, just kept his eyes on the road. Michael's 99 Ford F-350 wasn't the best handling vehicle to be in a car chase in, and the van had a considerable head start, but Jack grew up on these roads and knew them like the back of his hand. Michael kept watching the tracker app. The gap between them was getting smaller; would they get to the van before the van got to the boat? Where was the boat? How many people were in the van? He reached under his coat and felt his Glock model 20. How many times had he doubted the necessity of carrying it? How many times had he tried to leave it in its LifeLock case only to go back and put it on? He hoped Chief Upham and Commissioner Stryker would be able to help. The icon on the tracker app changed roads again.

"Jack, he just took the left onto Western Avenue."

Jack, still steadily focused, just kept his eyes on the road. Soon, that same intersection came into view. Jack let off the pedal a bit and let the natural drag of the truck slow him down a bit, only resting his foot gingerly on the brake pedal as he turned the steering wheel; when his truck was halfway through the sharp turn, he hit the accelerator pedal hard to the floor, drifting the large truck through the turn, narrowly missing the guard rail and sending Jarvis to the other side of the cab. Then it occurred to Jack where he was. He was rounding the same corner that Stephanie had been murdered on. A lump formed in his throat. "Not again," he thought to himself.

Paul was driving calmly, going just a bit over the speed limit but not enough to attract attention, but there wasn't a single other car to be seen. Except that set of headlights in his rear view mirror some distance back. The head lights looked similar to those of Jack Finn's truck, but he couldn't be too sure, many people around here had the same vehicles. With the roads so curvy, they were in and out of view in fractions of a second. He decided to start speeding more. Agent Rand felt the speed of the van pick up. She took advantage of the tossing and turning and exaggerated the rolling so she could be next to Melissa. She had a pulse, but slow. She cut the zip tie from Melissa's wrists and ankles. If she ever saw Michael again, he was going to buy him a drink for this damn crazy knife. The waiting game continued, not knowing where she was headed, or if anyone knew she was missing. Someone had to hear those shots. She hoped Andy was ok, but she feared the worst. As she replayed the moment in her head, she began to remember details that seemed to confuse her more. This guy had a suppressor, and two of those shots she heard sounded like her Glock 43; it had a shorter barrel, so it was louder. The other two shots sounded similar to hers but a bit different. Did Andy grab her gun?

"There it is, Jack; we got to be smart about this. We don't know how many guys are in that van. Kill your lights and pull into that parking place." Michael said as he pointed out a parking place right in front of Eventide. Jack didn't pull all the way in, leaving a bit of room to pull out in a hurry if need be. They were about 70 yards away. Michael pulled his Glock 20 from his holster. There was no need to rack it, he always kept a round in the chamber. They watched as Paul backed the van up between some trees and the Captain Fish Whale watch ticket booth.

"Jack, I am going to slowly get out and edge my way down the side of this building. I can't see anything from here."

Carla heard the van shut off, and Paul opened the driver's side door. She had two plans worked out in her head. Plan one, if he grabbed her first, she would let him carry her away from the van aways before attacking. She had to be careful; she did only have a knife with a five-inch blade. She had pulled it back into its spring-loaded holster on her wrist. It had enough force to pierce clothes and flesh, but this guy had a gun and another hostage. If she messed up, she and Melissa would surely be killed. Plan two, if he took Melissa, she would wait for him to come back for her and surprise him when he got back. The back door to the van opened, and the man grabbed Melissa. He put her up on his shoulder in a fireman's carry. He gave Melissa a slap on her butt and chuckled. He didn't even notice that Melissa's arms and legs were free.

It was a windy night, and the waterfront was active with noises of the waves crashing against the docks and shoreline. The docks answered, back an agitated clatter of the dock hardware grinding and binding against itself. The amber glow of a few streetlights provided enough light to see figures but no detail.

Michael had opened Jack's truck door and left it open to not make a sound. Jack and Jarvis sat in the truck and watched as Michael went out of sight, creeping down the side of the building. Suddenly, Jarvis's ears perked up, and he made a whimper. The wind had brought Melissa's scent to his nose. Jack made a motion to hold him while saying, "sssshhhh, easy bud." But Jarvis shot out of the truck and passed Michael, and headed towards the van aas Paul started walking down the ramp, it moved under his feet. The combination of his wound and Melissa on his shoulder, made him stumble but he caught himself. As he stepped onto the dock, he heard something, the patter of paws followed by a low, ominous growl coming up behind him. He reached for his gun and turned. Jarvis leaped up and bit Paul on the wrist, causing him to lose his gun overboard. He fell to the ground, with Melissa on top of him. Melissa faintly mumbled "Jack" when she hit the dock; she was coming to. Jarvis had let go of the wrist and started barking at Paul, trying to get another bite at something, but Paul planted a kick onto his chest, sending the dog overboard. Jarvis yelped in pain, then started splashing and clawing at the dock to try to get away from the cold salt water. Agent Rand had heard the dog barking and the splash and thought Paul may have thrown Melissa into the water in her unconscious state. She jumped out of the van, pulling the hood from her head. She saw Paul picking Melissa back up from the dock and putting her into a small boat. The boat started and pulled away, breaking the dock lines as it left. A gunshot rang out from behind her, followed by the sound of a bullet hitting the metal frame of the T-top of the boat just above Paul's head. She turned to see Michael running down the street into the parking lot.

"I am ok. I will get the dog; you guys go after the boat." Agent Rand called out.

Jack's boat was tied up over at The Harbor. They ran back to the truck and sped in that direction.

"He had a head start on us; how the hell are we going to catch him?" Michael said, looking out across the harbor.

"He will probably stay on the west side of Harbor Island and go to the east of Tumbler. There are enough boats and floats in the harbor to slow him down. Not to mention the wind and waves. That was just a little center console. Once we get *Red At Night* going, I can turn the lights on. That will make it easier for us to see and blind him a bit."

Jack drove around the head of the harbor and up Atlantic Avenue. Reaching 80 MPH while going past the Footbridge parking lot. He hoped nobody would be coming the other way or that no one would be crossing the street. His truck felt like it was air born as he crested the hill by the Catholic Church. Michael could see the small boat heading out in the moonlight. Jack drove right onto the dock and slammed on the brakes. The truck came to a stop, just short of the edge. They ran down the dock to the *Red At Night*. Michael leaped across the engine box, reached into the companionway door, and turned on the battery switch while Jack started the boat. They each cut the lines rather than untying them. Jack put the boat into gear and pinned the throttle, tracking the small center console. He looked over, and Michael was on the portside of the boat, holding on to the cabin's grab rails, working his way to the bow of the boat. The sea was turbulent, and the waves were peaking; the *Red At Night* danced on top of the white caps. Jack was concerned that the pounding and sudden pitching would cause Michael to fall off.

Melissa couldn't figure out why she couldn't see. She opened her eyes, but all she saw was black. Then her ears reported sounds of water rushing. She attempted a big breath, but something was in front of her mouth. She put her hand to her face and felt a cloth. She grabbed it, trying to pull it off, but didn't have the strength. She felt like she was hung over, but she knew she wasn't drunk. She had just been to Lizzy's prom. She and Carla were called to the bathroom, then the van, that guy, and a pinch on her neck. Her heart started racing; she was figuring out what happened. She had been drugged. She pulled again at the cloth on her face and got some of it to move. It was a hood or bag over her head.

Michael kneeled on the foredeck of the *Red At Night*, putting his weight on his right leg and his left knee up, then pulled out his Glock.

"Jack, turn on the Durabrites and blind the fucker. I don't want him able to return fire. He may have a gun on the boat."

The lights came on and lit up not only the center console but a bigger yacht in the distance. Michael held up his gun, placing his left elbow on his left knee to help steady his arms. The shot had to be around 100 to 120 yards. Both boats were moving, and Melissa was somewhere on that boat, but he couldn't see her, so he was clear to fire. He lined up his sight picture on Paul's back, and slowly squeezed the trigger.

Melissa could hear the gun shot then the boat swerved a bit. She saw a man down on his right knee, clutching his right buttocks. He pulled himself back up to a standing position and gave the boat more throttle. The boat was bouncing violently now, almost out of control. She picked herself up and looked out over the twin outboards. All she could see was the glaring light, but she knew who it was. Jack was coming for her. Considering the gunshot, she decided to duck back down and work on getting more mobility.

Michael knew Jack was at full throttle. The small boat had sped up, now making the gap bigger and harder since the boat was bouncing more violently. He took a deep breath and held it, lined up his sight picture as before, and found the rhythm that the small boat was bouncing too. He slowly squeezed the trigger, timing the shot according to the bounce. The shot rang out, and Michael could see the reward of his timing and marksmanship. Paul arched his back and fell back against the seat, grabbing out at anything to keep him up, bumping the throttle down as he fell. The *Red At Night* started gaining on the small craft.

Demitri Balfour was on the bridge of his yacht, talking to Paul on his cell phone, when he heard the shots, then Paul grimaced loudly in agony.

"Paul, Paul, what happened?"

He could see the small center console slow down and another boat with bright lights getting closer. These locals, these pitchfork rednecks, had destroyed his plan. Well, almost; he put the yacht in gear and set the autopilot. Then, took out his gun.

⁕⁕⁕⁕⁕⁕⁕⁕⁕⁕⁕

Michael came back into the cabin and yelled over the engine noise. "You are going to have to jump onto that boat. I am too damn old to do it and would end up missing."

Jack let Michael take the helm while he jumped up onto the starboard wash rail and held on to the davit. He could see Melissa up on all fours now, trying to stand and get to the helm. Michael could see a large yacht coming into view. He pulled up alongside the small craft. Jack made the leap into the boat. His landing was much more of a semi-controlled fall. Just as he got back up, more gunfire came. This time from ahead, from the yacht just in the distance. It had shot out one of his lights, probably to get a cleaner shot at them. The yacht was heading straight at them. Jack pinned the throttle, pointing the small boat towards the yacht. Jack grabbed Melissa off the deck, which was now slippery with Paul's blood, and jumped over the side with Melissa in his arms. Michael saw the action and brought the *Red At Night* up to where Jack and Melissa were now swimming. Well, Jack was swimming for both of them. The yacht was too concerned with the incoming small craft, trying to turn to avoid it, but it was too late. Just as Michael got Melissa on board, the small boat hit the large vessel. The explosion was enormous; it made Michael jump, then he could feel the heat and smell the rank burning of fiberglass. He stood staring in awe of the spectacle.

"Hey…. I am still down here!" Jack yelled at Michael. Michael had been distracted by the explosion, now bent down to get Jack out of the water. The Coast Guard arrived shortly along with Commissioner Stryker, but there was nothing anyone could do. The yacht was completely engulfed in flames and was taking on water.

Chapter 13

Police Chief Nick Upham was patrolling the Sprucewold area, by where Melissa lived. A man in dark clothing had been seen walking around the area. That call didn't alert him much; people often reported the most mundane things, like a hooded person walking around a neighborhood. The second call from another person who noticed someone walking around Melissa's house is what put him on alert. He knew she wasn't home; it was prom, and she and a few others were helping chaperone. He parked at the end of her driveway and walked up to the house; that way, if someone ran out, his dash cam would see them. Also, if Jarvis was home, a car coming up the driveway would make him bark, spooking anyone creeping around the place. As he walked up, everything looked normal. He continued his steps, then when he was just twenty-five yards away, he stopped dead in his tracks. "Was that a shadow he just saw in the window?" he thought to himself. He wasn't even sure he saw anything. Melissa had not yet taken his suggestion of adding more lights to the outside of the house, nor had she changed her inside lighting to motion sensing. He rested his left hand on his firearm. He didn't have reason to draw it yet, but his senses were telling him to be ready. He walked up onto the porch and checked the door. It was unlocked; was this Melissa leaving it unlocked, or was this someone who had picked the lock? He stepped in slowly, only to hear the floor creep as he put his weight on his right foot. "Damned old cottages," he muttered to himself. Then came a sharp pain to his head, and he fell to the floor.

"Sorry, Chief Upham, but I can't be found; coming into this house was a mistake for both of us," said the mysterious man in black. He left the house, closing the door behind him.

At the Maine Botanical Gardens, Lizzy had left the students to find out what was going on. She saw Lucy weeping over a body, when she got closer, she realized it was Sam. Before she could go to her side, she heard Agent Roberts groan her name.

"Carla and Melissa have been kidnapped. Your dad and Jack went after them, blue van," he spoke with agony. A police car and ambulance rolled onto the scene. Sergeant David Benner got out of his car and took charge.

"Where is Chief Upham?" Agent Roberts moaned.

"We don't know. He isn't answering his radio or his cell phone. Commissioner Stryker called me when he couldn't get a hold of the chief."

The EMTs tried to revive Sam, but he had lost too much blood. They waited for Lucy to let go before placing him on a stretcher and putting him into the ambulance. Agent Roberts' vest had stopped the bullets, but not without breaking his sternum; but, he was alive and could breathe. He was able to tell them about what had happened and what was going on. He told Sergeant Benner to stay off the radio. They loaded him into the ambulance next to Sam. Sergeant Benner found the gun by where Sam had been lying. He put on gloves and picked it up. He took it to his cruiser and ran the serial number; it came back to Agent Carla Rand, confirming what Agent Roberts had told him.

When Jack, Melissa, and Michael had come back in, they were taken to the police station too. The regional chief of the FBI, Special

Agent in Charge Chuck Tarling, had been called in and questioned them individually. Agent Tarling wanted to handle this personally since Agent Roberts, whom he questioned first in the hospital, had warned about possible moles in the agency. All the stories from Agent Roberts, Agent Rand, Michael, Jack, and Melissa fit together to get the big picture. He told them all there would be more questioning in the future and asked that Michael turn over his firearm just in case they found Paul's body and wanted to match forensics. Melissa was taken to the hospital for monitoring; Jack said he would be there shortly. Chief Nick Upham had reported that he had been assaulted at Melissa's house. No sign of the man in black clothing was ever found. Some thought that he was a diversion to what was really going on.

Before leaving, Jack and Michael stood outside of the police station. The wind was still blowing, and the ropes on the flagpole were slapping the side of the pole, accented by the sound of the metal shackle that hit on occasion.

"Well, Jack, a smarter man might know what to say right now, but I don't have a clue. I just want to get home and hold my kids and my wife."

"Michael, there ain't much to say. And at the same time, there is a lot that should be said. I just don't think we have the focus or the energy to process it now. All I can think to say is thank you."

Michael didn't know how to respond. He had shot and killed a man tonight. The man he shot was a bad man, but he had still taken a life. All those years in the Navy, all those hotspots he had been in with the SEALs, he had never once had to take a life.

"Like I said, Jack, I just want to get home and hold my wife and kids."

Jack took the repetition as a sign that Michael didn't want to talk. Jack really didn't want to talk much either, but he had too. Lucy would need to know how Sam died.

⚜

Jack was dropped off by one of the police at the Finn family compound. He walked up to his parents' door and could already hear Lucy inside. This door was usually warm and inviting, felt cold and almost had a force field pushing back at Jack. It was guilt, Jack knew Sam had given his life to save Melissa and Agent Rand. Melissa, who was now safe and who he would be sharing a life with. "She has to know." he said to himself. Jack overcame the forcefield and opened the door and walked inside. His mother was sitting next to Lucy, holding her while Lucy cried. His father stood above them; his eyes watery with tears as well. His father spoke first.

"What happened Jack, they say Sam was shot and someone tried to kidnap Melissa and Carla. What is going on."

"That is what happened, and they would have got away if not for Sam."

Jack told the whole story, how Sam had shot first and wounded the bad guy.

All Lucy could say was "My Sam, oh my Sam."

The Finn Family held each other remembering a great man.

Chapter 14

Anne woke lying beside Lucy, she had walked Lucy home and stayed with her overnight. She looked down to see Lucy's eyes opening and staring into nothingness. Anne wanted to ask how she was doing, but that question felt so obvious, yet she felt she needed to say something, then Lucy spoke.

"Mom, are we going to have breakfast this morning?"

"I hadn't planned on it; not sure anyone would be in the mood."

"I am in the mood, I need to do something, to move to get my mind off of things."

"I will go to the house and send out a text message, we will see how everyone feels about it. That will give you some time to get yourself together."

Anne Finn sent out a text to everyone, stating that they would still be making breakfast but would understand if people didn't feel up to it. To her amazement, everyone responded they would be over, she figured in times like this people need family and friends the most. She started getting things together when Lucy walked in and joined her in the kitchen; she didn't speak, she just went to work. Jack and Melissa pulled in, and Melissa went into the kitchen. She gave Lucy a hug, and the women all embraced for a bit. The Williams family arrived, then Carla Rand and Andy Roberts. The mood in the kitchen and outside was somber, mostly small talk, and nobody wanted to talk about the night before. They all sat down for breakfast; Russell stood up to address the group. He looked around the table, all looking up to him. He really didn't have any words. There was none; nothing could cover the field of emotions that he and all these people were feeling. He forced a bit of a smile and said, "Let's eat."

They all ate quietly, taking in the comfort of the food and each other's company. While eating, Jack nudged Melissa, then whispered in her ear; she nodded in compliance. After everyone was full and leaning back in their chairs, Jack spoke up.

"Melissa and I have an announcement to make. Some of you already know, but now we want to make it official." He paused and took Melissa's hand. "Melissa is pregnant."

The announcement brought a bit of joy to the somber mood. There were handshakes and hugs all around. After they settled a bit, the men took the dishes into the kitchen and started cleaning up. Melissa had just sat down with the women and noticed Lucy walking by herself down to the dock. She gave Anne a quick look, as if to ask if she should follow, Anne spoke softly, "Let's give her a moment."

Lucy walked down the hill and down onto the dock. She sat down, cross legged, and took a long, deep breath. It was a warm and sunny morning, and the wind from last night had stopped and the air was now still.

"Sam, so this is day one without you. I cried all night; I don't even know how I am awake right now. The clothes that you were wearing before changing into your tux are still on the floor. They were the first things I saw when I walked into the house. Normally, I would have taken a picture of them and sent it to you. Now, I wish you would be here to leave more stuff out," she said, while starting to cry. She reached into her pocket and pulled out the black velvet box that was stained with Sam's blood. She opened the box and looked at the ring. It was simple and elegant. A single diamond on a gold band. She slid it on the ring finger of her left hand. It fit perfectly. "Oh Samuel, my Sam." She pressed her hands to her face, and the tears came in full force now. She heard footsteps coming, and then her mother sat to one side and Melissa sat on the other. Both held her and didn't say a word.

After the dishes were done, the men came back out and joined the women outside. Anne, Lucy, and Melissa walked up from the dock, and they all sat there talking about Sam and the man he was. Agent Chuck Tarling called Andy Roberts to let him know that the Coast Guard had recovered the bodies of several people. One had a 9mm gunshot wound to the shoulder and two more 10mm gunshot wounds to the right buttocks and his back, breaking the spin in two. Andy relayed this message.

"That means Sam, did get a piece of him with my gun." Agent Rand announced.

"Yeah, and Michael shot him in the ass before he died. That asshole died in pain," chided Russell.

The week seemed to drift by as in a gray haze. Melissa finally took Nick's advice and put more motion sensing lighting outside of the house, and all the inside lighting was changed to motion sensing as well. Nobody had seen the mysterious man in black clothing since that night. Everyone took care of Lucy, Jack especially; he had been through this before.

They held a Celebration of Life at The Harbor for Sam. The story of Sam's bravery was passed on and on, Sam would be remembered as a hero. After the celebration the Finn and Williams family joined Lucy at the Finn family dock while she spread Sam's ashes into the water. Lucy spent many nights sitting on the dock, looking out over the water.

Agent Roberts kept them aware of the investigation; he was back on full duty and was part of the team that investigated Demetri Balfour. They inspected his warehouse and found records of all the sales of his human trafficking. For weeks, there were sting operations busting people using Balfour's website. Agent Rand was cleared of all charges. The Coast Guard, with assistance from the FBI, had recovered more bodies from the sunken yacht. With no records of Balfour and with the bodies being burned and submerged, identifying them was nearly impossible. The FBI forensics lab would be working for months trying to identify them.

172

Chapter 15

The salt air never smelled better to Melissa; she stood next to Russell, arms interlocking, her white dress gently waving in the breeze. They had hung a makeshift curtain around the opening to Jack's cabin. Russell had worked on it for weeks, knitting a net, while Anne tied Gerbera daisies to it. Lizzy and Abigail stood just outside of the cabin, while Anne, Lucy, and other friends and family stood making an aisle way to the stairs that led to the platform Jack had built; it looked wonderful. The white platform was trimmed with driftwood, sea glass, and shells. She heard the *Overtime* pull up and tie up on the port side of *Red At Night*. Jack stepped onboard of his boat and walked up onto the platform. Michael followed, with Chris Pratt behind him. Melissa was a little surprised by the sudden change. She had thought for sure that Josh was going to be a groomsman. Then she got her answer; she had agreed to let Jack choose the song she would walk down the aisle to, and Josh started singing Garth Brooks' "To Make You Feel My Love."

Russell and Melissa started walking forward, and Lizzy and Abigial pulled back the net curtain and followed behind them. Russell walked Melissa up the stairs and to Jack. He turned to his son, smiled, and spoke. "Take good care of her; she is a great woman."

"I will, dad." Jack responded. Russell left the platform, and the minister walked up and stood before Jack and Melissa.

"We are gathered here today….." The minister started the ceremony. Melissa stood there, looking at Jack, her soon to be husband and the soon to be father of their child. It was just a year ago that they had met at this very spot. Jack had rescued her from the water and from a loveless life. They had built a relationship that people dreamed about, what people wrote novels about, and done so in a year. She had a family now, The Finn and Williams Family. She now knew love; this is love.

"Do you, Melissa, take this man to be your lawfully wedded husband?"

"I do."

"Do you, Jack, promise to……..

Jack heard the preacher's words, but he was counting all the smiles Melissa had given him up to this point, starting with the first one on this very boat at this very spot. The crinkling of her nose at the smell of his hoodie, the listening to him carefully to understand his Maine accent. The smile she gave him when she told him she was pregnant, and the smile she gave him when he had saved her from being kidnapped, and now standing across from him. There will be many more to come. They had love; this was love.

"Do you, Jack, take this woman to be your lawfully wedded wife?"

"I do."

"I now pronounce you Mr. and Mrs. Jack Finn."

The *Red At Night* pulled up to the dock to the cheers of the crowd. *Overtime* and *Old Smoke* pulled in behind them. The Harbor never looked so good; there were beautiful white garlands with Gerbera daisies weaved into them floating in the breeze, bright white tablecloths flapping like flags. Even the ramp going up had been decorated. As they walked up to the dance floor, Jack couldn't get over the mix of people. Robert Downey Jr. was standing next to Clive Farrin; Clive looked to be pointing out points in the harbor.

Taylor Swift was talking with Hazel Westin and some other of Lizzy's friends. Andy Roberts and Carla Rand were talking to Ed Sheeran. All of their friends were dressed up and looking nice.

They walked to the center of the dance floor, and the crowd went silent. Jack and Melissa stood, facing each other, smiling at each other, Melissa giggling a bit, waiting for the music to start.

"What did you pick?" Melissa asked.

"You will see, I got a little help."

Then a familiar strumming of a guitar was heard, with Ed Sheeran playing. He started singing, "We were born before the wind."

"Aaahhh, Into the Mystic, good choice." said Melissa

"May I have this dance, Mrs. Finn?"

"Now and forever, Mr. Finn."

They started dancing together, completely lost in each other's eyes. They almost didn't notice when Taylor Swift joined in with the singing and guitar, followed by Josh on the last verse. After the song ended, they gave a bow to the crowd and welcomed them onto the dance floor. When the first set of songs ended, the DJ prompted everyone to take a seat for the maid of honor and best man speeches.

Lizzy took the microphone from the DJ and stood in the middle of the dance floor. "There is a pile of notebook paper beside my desk at home because I have started this speech so many times and the words just didn't seem to fit. How do I describe what you two have? Uncle Jack, you have the biggest heart. You loved me and my brother like we were your own. You made us feel special whenever we were with you. Like we were the only two kids in the world. I know you make Melissa feel the same way, and I know she makes you feel that way. I may be young, but I know you two will love each other as long as the tide changes." Lizzy then passed the microphone to her father.

"Melissa, I could go on about how you have found a great man. Jack is the closest thing I have to a brother, and he means a lot to me. I could stand here and tell you not to hurt him and to treat him right. I could tell you to love him with everything you got. But I won't; you already know you have a great man, you would never hurt him, and I know you will treat him right and that you will love him with a passion most people will never understand. I know this because that is how you love everyone in your life. Russell, Anne, Lucy, and my family. You are truly one of the greatest people I know. I wish you both a great life together, and Jack….. if you ever hurt her, I will throw you overboard!"

Everyone cheered and toasted. They dined on baked stuffed lobster and steaks. After the meal, the dancing and partying continued and of course, karaoke, in which Josh and Talyor stole the show with their duet of "Islands in the Stream."

Jack and Melissa walked down the ramp and into Jack's boat. The sun was starting to set, and the sky was turning from yellow to orange to red. Jack untied the lines, and they both waved up to the crowd, as Jack slowly backed away from the dock.

⁂

Demetri Balfour opened the sliding door of his hotel room and stuck the muzzle of his Beretta REC7 DI sniper rifle through the opening. The TV in the room upstairs had just got louder, but he wouldn't let that distract him. He could see both Melissa and Agent Rand. He knew he could kill those two at least, then just start pulling the trigger until the gun was empty. He would leave Jack to mourn his new wife and unborn baby, but maybe he could kill that Michael Williams or Jack's parents. He had 20 rounds to work with, and his prey had no idea what was about to happen. He placed the cross hairs on the center of Melissa's head and slowly pulled the trigger.

"Click."

The gun did nothing. He checked the safety, then cycled the action. One round came out of the ejection port, and he lined up on Melissa again.

"Click."

Behind him came the sound of a revolver cocking. He turned to see a man dressed all in black with shady glasses on.

"I would love to shoot you right now, but the sound would disturb my daughter's special day. Instead, I am going to tape you up and gag you. If you are lucky, someone will find you before you die; if not, they will eventually smell your rotting corpse."

He struck Balfour on the back of the head with the butt of the revolver. He ziptied Balfour's hands and feet behind his back and put heavy duty duct tape over Balfour's mouth. As he left the room, he placed the "Do not disturb sign" on the door handle. He walked down the hall, noticing the cameras as he discarded his gloves in a trash can.

Jerry Farnham

Epilogue

Jack wiped the sweat from Melissa's face while she held his hand. She squeezed it so hard, he thought she might break a couple of his fingers, but he didn't dare complain. He looked over her belly as the doctor raised his head from Melissa's gown, holding the baby.

"Would you like to cut the cord?" The doctor asked.

Jack couldn't speak; he just nodded and slowly took the scissors from the nurse's hand. The nurse then held a portion of the umbilical cord between two hands for Jack to cut. He knew from the classes that neither the baby nor mother could feel this, but he was worried Melissa would jump or the baby would scream when he cut it. The scissors were sharp and cut through quickly. The doctor then placed the baby in Melissa's arm, and she and Jack cried happy, loving tears at the sight of their new baby boy.

Jack helped clean the baby up while one of the nurses helped Melissa get cleaned up. The staff checked the baby briefly to make sure it was perfectly healthy. Soon, the baby was back in Melissa's arms. She gave Jack a nod that she was ready for the family. He got up and opened the door, and called them in. Russell, Anne, and Lucy came into the room.

"It's a boy," said Melissa. She caught Jack's eyes, and he smiled back in approval of what she was thinking. "Everyone, meet Samuel Russell Finn."

About the Author

I was raised in Boothbay Harbor, the son of a lobsterman. I grew up on a lobster boat going sternman every summer from age six until I left to serve my country in the US Navy. I returned to civilian life in 2007 taking several jobs and going back to School before settling in Gorham Maine with my wife and 2 kids. I enjoy writing, unprofessionally, for www.DowneastBoatForum.com, archery, working on my boat *Tip Jar*, or my Jeep named MeatLug, and most of all I love being a husband and father.

Connect with me online:

http://www.jerryfarnham.com/